B

Delicate Dames

"WHEN FOUR RICH, old, bored and fiendish female neighbours get together over cocktails and canapés in their high-end senior condos, you'd expect the conversation to be about delicately plotting the next visit to a concert or a fashion show. But not these Dames. They plot murders while nibbling on caviar. Having selected a well-deserving prey, they stalk and sleuth him with a combination of canny intelligence and comical incompetence like four drunken Jack The Rippers in drag. Intertwined in this lunacy, however, is the emerging poignancy of their real lives, their loneliness, their lost loves, and the stark cruelty of death.

"As time goes on the Dames face the losses of their pasts, find new hope for their futures, and above all else thrive through the strength of their powerful 4-way friendship ... and of course, their totally indestructible sense of humor. This wickedly funny story will have you howling with laughter on one page, in tears of sympathy on the next, and will grip your attention so tightly that I promise, you won't stop reading until 'the end.' A superb tribute to Barbara Grengs' highly developed sense of the ridiculous and sheer story-telling genius."

—Suzan St. Maur, author of *Mischieverse: Rude humor that laughs at life's irritations*

"RICH, SAUCY, BORED, and full of beans,
The Dames devise inventive means
To "off" deserving senior males
Whose lives are weighed and judged as 'fails.'
The story, picaresque at first,
May make you laugh until you burst;
But then you find its theme depends

On growing old with best of friends.
Evoking laughter, thoughtful tears,
It tells the story of our years."
   —Lee Johnson, author of *Poetria Nova*

The Toby Martin Series

"I HAVE GROWN up reading and writing reviews for these humorous books about the mystery solving sleuth, Toby Martin. As Toby's character has grown over the years I too, have grown with her. Sharing in many similarities, especially the curly hair. This was such a heartfelt way to end the *Toby Martin: Pet Detective* era. We say farewell to Toby but we will always cherish the feisty playfulness she brought to this extraordinary series, written by an even more extraordinary woman."
   — Ellie Capistrant, 16, a student at Roseville Area High School, Roseville, MN

"THIS IS A HIGHLY FUNNY BOOK in an obvious way that can't be denied. Unlike some other books, the language used isn't what you would expect to hear from a book, but what you expect to hear in real life. That factor helps you to really visualize the story as you are reading it. A fantastic job by a great author!"
   — Oliver Prowse, age 10, Cheshire, England

"THIS BOOK IS FANTASTIC! I could not stop reading it and was told off by my mom for still being up at two in the morning. Also I read it three times and I am still reading the book. To put it together in one sentence: it was impossible to put down."
   — Alice Dobson, age 11, Düsseldorf, Germany

"A GIRL HARRY POTTER! Toby is spunky and Mrs. Trattles is snake-like. A fun read!"
   — Caleb Twiggs, age 12, Roseville, Minnesota

Delicate Dames

by Barbara Grengs

Cambridge Books

an imprint of

WriteWords, Inc.

CAMBRIDGE, MD 21613

𝕮𝖆𝖒𝖇𝖗𝖎𝖉𝖌𝖊 𝕭𝖔𝖔𝖐𝖘 is a subsidiary of:

Write Words, Inc.
2934 Old Route 50
Cambridge, MD 21613

ISBN 978-1-61386-409-8

Fax: 410-221-7510

Bowker Standard Address Number: 254-0304

DEDICATION

For all the Dames in my life, delicate and otherwise.

THE DAMES

Margaret Thompson aka Closer: Widowed three times with no children, Margaret inherited oodles of cash, stocks, and property which allowed her a high-end lifestyle. Even though she was in her seventies with several cosmetic surgeries under her belt, she attracted significant attention from men, attractive and otherwise.

Karen Bradley aka Decrease: Eighty-something, thrice divorced, Karen made her way through life by marrying well. Generous settlements allowed her to live a life of luxury in her dotage or as she liked to say, her "doltage." Add four children, multiple grandchildren, her hobby of knitting and life was good.

Susan Waverly aka Browser: Youngest of the Dames at sixty-six, Susan never married. Instead of a husband or children, she focused on a stellar career in technology. Unfortunately, she was crippled in a terrible car crash and confined to a wheelchair, but her savvy technological skills and a sizable award from the driver's insurance allowed her to live in luxury.

Lynn Cruz aka Toxic: Chubby and crazy about cats, gardening, and cheesecake, Lynn found herself a widow with means and two children to raise. Her deceased husband was a renowned cardiologist who dropped dead of a heart attack. Now in her seventies, she found herself exploring a new, hip, persona. And yes, she'd had a hip replaced.

CHAPTER 1

Dames and Games

They discovered they could be killers. Gentle. Delicate. Killers. More importantly they discovered they could love one another. And it was all because of the Game.

The women had many things in common: They were filthy rich, bored, game-loving old broads who lived in an upscale senior high rise that offered all the amenities for the entitled elderly: a beauty parlor, exercise room, swimming pool, tennis courts plus an on-call attractive Hispanic masseur named Carlos, and a not so attractive dog walker named Bruce.

Canasta, poker, bridge, Scrabble, board games, even TV game shows occupied their mornings and afternoons, but no game took precedence over *The Game*, aka "Pop Goes the Weasel." This is where they discussed their next "project," while sipping tea and nibbling various fattening desserts brought to them from the gourmet restaurant on the bottom floor of their building. Once a "project" was completed and the obituary created, they celebrated by upgrading the beverages to gin and tonics in the summer and vintage red wines in the winter.

Their "clients," the term the Dames preferred, were elderly males deserving premature death, if only by a few months or years. They were elderly after all. Thus far, they had delicately "eliminated" two philanderers and an immoral attorney who had fleeced several of their friends in a real estate scam. They were looking to "up their game."

Delicate Dames did not "kill" indiscriminately; they believed their clients deserved their early demise, at least that's what the old girls told themselves whenever their consciences were pricked which was seldom and only after a few drinks. Then the arguments turned to evil thoughts vs. evil deeds and the difference between them.

For the sake of argument, several opined that "lusting in one's heart" was just as immoral as actually "doing *IT*." Margaret Thompson, the biggest devotee of "doing IT," argued, "If it's just as wrong to think evil as it is to do evil, you might as well have the fun." She also owned stock in Nike, whose motto "Just do it!" was supposedly inspired by killer Gary Gilmore's last words. Thus, one of the bylaws for the Game was drinking in moderation at least until *IT* was accomplished, thereby eliminating the theological blather.

They met in Margaret's 2500 square foot two bedroom, three bathroom flat decorated right out of *Architectural Digest*. With lots of glass, birch wood and expensive modern art that no one, except Margaret, understood or liked for that matter, Margaret's fifth floor apartment reminded the Dames of being in Manhattan, not a bad fantasy considering they lived in Mendota Heights, a southern suburb of St. Paul, Minnesota. A large wrap around balcony bordered the flat on two sides so the Dames could sit and look over the Minnesota river and the St. Paul skyline while sipping their beverages when the weather allowed.

In Minnesota the weather could be problematic: blizzards, flash floods, tornadoes, all possible in the Land of 10,000 Lakes. A common remark was, "If you don't like the weather now, just wait a few hours." In some cases, a few minutes would suffice.

Today the Dames were meeting inside because the weather forecasters were predicting severe thunderstorms, a common event in June, along with weddings. Both often lead to disaster. And since it was Project Planning Time they were sipping iced tea in beautiful crystal goblets. The G and Ts would come later, once IT was accomplished.

"Girls, girls, time to stop gabbing and listen up!" Margaret bellowed. Like Rumpole's wife in the BBC '90s sit-com, Margaret was the epitome of "she who must be obeyed." Wearing purple capris and a striped cotton knit top, she was attractive and sexy even though she was well into her seventies. Margaret was a natural leader and a not-so-natural blonde. Now in her golden years, Margaret collected a variety of blonde very expensive wigs. Today's choice was a short, tousled style a la Meg Ryan that made her look more like a college student than a woman in her seventies. Of course, her trim body with surgically enhanced perky breasts added to the illusion.

In college she had been president of her sorority and went on to marry well three times although she never had children. Each time a husband would "move on," Margaret's euphemism for dying, she would inherit a bundle. Of the four women in the Delicate Dames, Margaret was the richest with Susan a close second. She was also the most vain. A veteran of cosmetic surgery, Margaret looked to be fifty and fit--a powerful weapon against impotent, wheezing, cardio-challenged geezers. When all other means failed, Delicate Dames brought in Margaret to finish the project, thus her nickname, 'Closer.' When Margaret bellowed, the girls eventually stopped their gossiping and gave her their full attention, well, almost their full attention.

"Shush, ladies," Karen whispered, not missing a stitch in her lacy shell pattern. Karen Bradley, a matronly type who knit her way through three marriages, four children and their subsequent progeny, gifted everyone with multicolored lap robes, afghans, hats, ill-fitting sweaters, and itchy socks. The grandbabies were bootied up their booties.

She and her mother even knit her first wedding dress, a complicated pattern with many buttons. *Knitting Knews* featured that unusual dress, showing Karen to be a beautiful, but conservatively dressed bride. No cleavage, no bare arms or back.

Unsurprisingly, the wedding night was problematic, like so many of them are. The reception over, toasts given and forgotten, guests stumbling home, Karen and her groom, Blake, went eagerly to the bridal suite. While engaging in brief foreplay and having no success extricating Karen from her elaborate knit dress, Blake called room service to deliver a sharp scissors ASAP. Once he had that scissors, he was a mad man, cutting off every button until she was standing there in her crocheted camisole and panties. Hours and hours of work destroyed just like that. She cried for days. No one was sure if it was because of the dress or the sex, but from that point on, she vowed never to spend a lot of energy on her husband's sexual needs, or money on yarn.

Even though the weather was warm and humid, Karen dressed in a bright Kelly green cable-stitched long-sleeved cardigan several sizes too small, Karen demurely pulled down her plaid straight skirt that tended to ride up. She also adjusted her Spanx in an effort to control the bulge above said skirt. Instead of that pesky muffin top, Karen sported a pound cake. Because she was always chilly and didn't want to display her flabby upper arms, Karen had a complete wardrobe of garishly colored hand-knit sweaters either too large or too small.

Thoughtful, soft-spoken, eighty-something, Karen was the voice of reason in the group; she also had the most creative ideas when it came to actual "projects." According to the Dames, her most creatively orchestrated "death" involved the previously mentioned immoral real estate attorney who happened to have severe asthma caused by dog dander. Karen made an appointment to see him, regarding a bogus home purchase, wearing a too-small, sweater knit with yarn spun from Samoyed dog hair that she found at a garage sale. She discreetly brushed against him when he ushered her into his tastefully decorated plush office. He wheezed and wheezed, gasping that he needed the inhaler in his top desk drawer. She ignored him. Karen left a trail of white on dark red and sage green oriental rugs while wisps of Sammy fur settled on the highly polished mahogany antiques. It was only a matter of minutes before said attorney was gasping for breath.

Karen smiled and thanked him for his time, then quietly left the office without calling 911. Because matronly elderly women are seldom noticed, no one was even aware of her exit. The only person who did notice the dog hair was the elderly cleaning woman who was also invisible.

Karen's moniker: 'Decrease.'

"Just a sec, Margaret, I need to log out," said Susan Waverly, the nerdy, science-geek who never married or had children. Instead of kids, Susan birthed several computer software programs that made her a ton of money back in the eighties. Only sixty-six, Susan was the youngest of the group and the least into fashion. She wore fresh-from-the-dryer sweat pants and t-shirts; today's ensemble included a bright gold U of M tee, with Goldie Gopher holding a football, and faded black sweatpants with a hole in the knee. If there were a Dames Frump Off, Susan would win hands down with Karen's coming in a close second. With her gray-streaked naturally curly dark brown hair in an unbecoming ponytail and dark rimmed glasses slipping down her nose, Susan was seldom seen with makeup or without her laptop. The Dames thought she was surgically attached to the damn thing. Her women friends and her beloved technology replaced husband and children, although rumor had it that she once had a fiancé who dumped her.

Unfortunately, Susan was disabled in a car accident caused by a drunk driver, making her the least mobile of the group, but that wasn't a huge problem because she was somewhat reclusive. When she did need to leave the building, she used her modified van. The accident also left her with a sizable settlement, making her the second most wealthy of the group. With all the services available to the girls, including Carlos's magic massage, Susan was able to live a luxurious life without ever having to lift a finger, all within the confines of a wheelchair. Actually, several very expensive wheelchairs.

The Dames depended on her for research because most of them didn't know or care beans about technology. They could barely use their cell phones. All the girls really wanted was to use the remote to find the right channel or maybe access their e-mail or Google their old lovers and ex-husbands.

The occasional consulting job provided Susan with the money to feed her state of the art technology addiction. It was Susan who had hacked into the attorney's medical records to uncover his severe allergies. Thus, her nickname, Browser. She was indispensable to the Dames' success.

"Please pass the fruit," Lynn Cruz said demurely, though her demure persona was taking a hit because she was learning to swear. Normally she would have demanded the turtle cheesecake, but she was on a diet. Known as Toxic because of her knowledge of poisonous plants, Lynn completed the team. As a young college student in the fifties, she gave up her ambitions of becoming a doctor to get married. Big mistake. Instead of becoming a doctor, she opted for nursing. Lynn worked her ass off to support her husband while he went on to get his specialty in cardiology. After he gained wealth and professional and social status, he went through the predictable mid-life crisis and ran off with his beautiful bimbo receptionist to live in Europe.

"Finish raising the children, will you? And by the way, sell the house as soon as possible. I could use the cash." His final words, literally, as he dropped over dead in Lynn's driveway, leaving her a very wealthy widow and the bimbo a minuscule blip on the radar.

Autopsy results showed a massive heart attack, such delicious irony, because Lynn considered the cardiologist heartless. The Dames weren't positive, but they suspected Lynn eliminated the narcissist since she was a master gardener and grew digitalis or foxglove, a known poison. Ever since her husband "moved on," Lynn filled her emptiness with rich food and animal rescues. Her gardening was now confined to elaborate deck plantings and a spare bedroom/greenhouse devoted to exotic tropicals. Since becoming part of the Dames, however, she felt her life had purpose, and she was beginning to drop a few pounds and a few cats, a good thing for all concerned. Her rose silk print blouse and white linen pants showcased her weight loss beautifully.

"Finally, we can get down to it. Hear, hear. Delicate Dames, let the good times begin.

Remember to name the client and give a brief description of his misdeeds. We'll then give the nominations to Browser to work her magic. At our next meeting we'll make our decision and decide on a plan. Okay, girls, any questions? Comments?"

"Oh, darn, I dropped a stitch," Karen said as she started to unravel the last sequence of stitches in her afghan.

"Put the damn thing down and pay attention," Lynn said as she chomped several strawberries in a single bite, red juice running down her double chin. "Shit, I've just dribbled on my blouse. I wore this color, knowing you'd have strawberries," she said, grinning at Margaret.

"As long as you keep the dribbles confined to your blouse," Karen smirked, looking up from her knitting.

"Finished with the kibitzing, girls? Now who would like to begin?" Margaret smiled and looked out at her dear friends.

"I'll start," said Susan. "I've been following the case of the sleazy used car dealer, Henry Beckler, who made millions, squandered the money living the high life with his mistresses and multiple homes, and now he's declared bankruptcy and is refusing to pay child support and alimony to all his ex-wives. He's also had three DUI citations. If anyone deserves elimination it would be Henry, but I just don't know how we'd get to him."

"No judgments, Susan, we'll discuss practical issues once we've made our choice," Margaret said, making sure the rules were followed.

"I'll go next," Lynn said. "This one is closer to home. I was having lunch with Mr. Miller and his cronies the other day."

"Is he the slimy bald guy or the one with the hair plugs?" Margaret asked.

"The one with the hair plugs. In my opinion, the hair plugs alone should make him a serious contender."

"I prefer hair plugs to the Trump comb-over any day," Karen said. Lynn flashed her a dirty look for interrupting.

"Anyway he was bragging about running down a cat with his Porsche. After he killed the cat, he stopped the car to check for damage as if a cat could cause damage to his precious Porsche. He told me he took it to the car wash immediately to clean off the blood and fur. Disgusting. To think someone could deliberately cause pain and suffering to an innocent animal. I tell you, if I had some arsenic on me, that shit would be history!"

"I can't believe you're equating Mr. Miller's misdeeds with Henry's. Get real," Karen said, once again picking up her needles and pointing them menacingly at Lynn. "You and your cats."

"You and your knitting."

"At least my yarn doesn't smell like cat pee," Karen said.

"Well, fuck me," Lynn said because she just discovered the f-bomb and swearing in general.

"That's fuck you, Lynn. If you're going to swear, at least get it right," Karen said, laughing.

"You'd probably have evil thoughts, too, if Mr. Miller grabbed your precious knitting and unraveled that afghan you've been working on for the past two months. I just know it." Lynn always tried to have the last word.

"Girls, girls, focus." Margaret gently tapped her goblet to get their attention. It tinkled the way fine crystal should. "Karen, it's your turn. Who is your nominee?"

"So many men, so little time. Well, I've given a great deal of thought to my nomination, unlike some others in the group." Karen looked accusingly at Lynn. Lynn responded with an obscene gesture.

"Here's the deal. Polly, my granddaughter goes to this sweet little grade school in Shoreview and a custodian at the school, a sixty-two year old man named Charles Goodwin, has just been arrested for installing cameras in the girls' restrooms so he can watch the little girls go potty. I mean how awful is that? When the police went to his home, they found child porn sites on his computer and movies of little girls in compromising positions. I've talked to my daughter about having Polly go to the Montessori school close to their home, just to get her away from that awful situation. At least he's in jail. Now that's a man who should be exterminated and maybe not so gently."

"Thanks, Karen. Well, I guess the last nomination's mine. I'm going to up the ante.

Let me see, should I nominate a slimy politician, a philandering retired professional athlete, or a drug-using has-been entertainer?" Margaret paused for effect, putting a carefully manicured pink nail to her chin. "How about a priest right here in the Twin Cities?" The girls gasped in unison.

"Give us dirt, Margaret," Susan said. "This should be fun."

"Well, for starters, Father Peter Flynn embezzled thousands from his parish; then he fiddled with young men and lied about it."

"Peter, great name for a 'fiddler,'" Lynn said in between mouthfuls. "Sort of puts the musical *Fiddler on the Roof* in a new light," she continued, laughing. The rest of the Dames giggled in support. "We could rename the musical *Diddler on the Roof.*"

"Focus, ladies. The Diocese has put him 'out to pasture' at St. Mark's University. Here is a picture of the not so good father." Margaret passed the picture to the Dames.

"Weak chin. My father always warned me about men with weak chins," Karen commented.

"Too bad you didn't listen to him. You could have avoided a couple of those bad marriages," Lynn said, getting the last word as usual.

Karen continued her knitting, not taking the bait. "He's better looking than I expected and older. I suppose the doting grandfather persona helped lure in young men," Karen said as she sipped her iced tea.

"There you have it, girls. Father Peter Flynn: hypocrisy, degradation, all in the name of the Lord. Now to summarize," Margaret continued. "Susan, you've nominated Henry Beckler, the narcissistic used car dealer, Lynn, Mr. Miller, the cat killer, Karen the pedophile custodian, and now my nomination of the profligate priest. Well, that's quite a motley crew, ladies. Susan will do as much research as possible about each nominee and report back to us next week. Remember, ladies, it's okay to snoop on your own. Check out phobias, allergies, medications, anything that could help us in the 'extermination.' Be sure to keep track of your observations, however trivial, and we'll compare notes at our next meeting. The Delicate Dames' weekly meeting is adjourned."

"See you on Sunday for poker," Margaret said.

"Better bring the big bucks, girls, cause I'm going to kick your butts," Lynn commented as she stabbed another strawberry with her fork.

Karen stared at her and wondered about the effectiveness of using one of her knitting needles to poke her friend or stab Charles Goodwin, the pedophile who victimized her granddaughter's classmates.

CHAPTER 2

Vetting a Sleaze

"Karen, what did you think of Lynn's inappropriate nomination? A cat killer, come on, how ridiculous is that?" Susan chuckled while she worked on her computer the morning after the meeting. The girls always made many phone calls to discuss the nominees and the nominators prior to the actual decision. Susan was actually researching Mr. Miller as she spoke to Karen on the phone. Technological multi-tasking was one of her specialties. She could watch her morning soaps, research a nominee, and talk on the phone, all at the same time, although sometimes she tended to confuse the soap opera sleaze with her research.

Susan's 1700 square foot flat was designed to accommodate her disability and her extensive technology needs. Her expansive and luxurious living room decorated in soft earth tones also served as a media center. Karen could watch hundreds of channels, surf the web, listen to jazz, or wheel into her gourmet kitchen to prepare a meal.

Then there was Susan's huge master bath designed specifically for her needs. She could pamper herself with the most cutting edge features, including a glassed in shower with specially designed shower heads at the appropriate height. She could program the temperature and the water pressure to suit her. When finished, she could wheel into a drying niche where warm air would dry her body and her hair. All she had to do was get dressed, which was easy for her because she didn't care how she looked.

Susan was the only Dame who actually cooked. Her specialties were stir fries and healthy salads. For the rest, cooking consisted of cutting up fruit, heating up frozen dinners and making drinks. On occasion one of them would go slumming and check out Trader Joe's on Randolph and Lexington. The store provided cheap cut flowers, a nice selection of appetizers including *sushi,* and a wide variety of gourmet cheese, for "unexpected company." Most days they ate at "their" restaurant or ordered in from "Gourmet to Go," a take-out delivery service from several high quality local restaurants or bistros.

"Wait a minute. I think I found something really juicy about Mr. Miller. Oh my god, you won't believe this."

"Enlighten me, Susan," Karen said as she helped herself to Cheerios and cut up fruit.

"Make sure this time you're not telling us about one of your soaps like you did before. Poor Mr. Johnson almost ended up exterminated because you accused him of having sex with his Doberman."

"Yeah, yeah, my bad. He was so creepy he might have fallen for the Doberman, and that would have been animal abuse. Too early for my programs, but this could be right up there with the Doberman." Susan laughed devilishly.

* * *

Meanwhile Lynn arranged a luncheon date with Mr. Miller, the cat killer and hair plugger. It was he who suggested Costello's, the posh Italian restaurant and deli just a few blocks from their high rise, not a bad idea considering her gal pals would be eating at the in-house gourmet cafe. She needed privacy for the meeting.

On the day of their "date," Margaret acted as wardrobe,

hair, and makeup consultant, a necessity if Lynn was to make a good impression. At Margaret's urging, Lynn chose a fashionable taupe silk Eileen Fisher pants suit. Lynn had just had her hair done that morning also at Margaret's suggestion. She was looking good.

"Ah, Mr. Miller, what a delight to see you again," Lynn said as she cozied up to the octogenarian who was seated at a table for two facing the deck and river. Mr. Miller grunted a bit as he stood up to shake her hand. The grunt was a familiar sound for Lynn, because she and her friends made similar sounds when they got up or sat down. It was an embarrassing affliction for the elderly. Sometimes the sounds were even accompanied by fragrances.

Mr. Miller had obviously dressed for the occasion. His sport coat was pressed and so was his shirt; nothing, however, could make up for the hair plugs. Lynn couldn't help staring at the obviously phony hair. She actually felt rather sorry for him because he did make an effort to impress her. Lynn almost succumbed to his efforts until she remembered his propensity for "catricide."

Mr. Miller stood up and pulled out Lynn's chair. "Always the gentleman," Lynn purred, feigning admiration.

Just as they were getting ready to order, the restaurant's owner, Marco Costello, sauntered by and whispered in Mr. Miller's ear. Lynn heard just a bit of the conversation: "Send her by around three tomorrow afternoon." Mr. Miller nodded in agreement.

"Sounds intriguing, Mr. Miller," Lynn said as she unwrapped her silverware from the white linen napkin. Lynn was starving and eyed the bread basket with unadulterated lust, like her cats when she brought home a rotisserie chicken. Apparently Mr. Miller felt the same way because he grabbed two pieces of baguette and slathered them with honey butter before Lynn even had a chance. Then he took a huge gulp of his dirty martini.

"Nothin' to be concerned about, girlie. I'm sendin' my

grand niece to interview for a job with Francesco in the deli," he said between mouthfuls. "She's home for the summer and needs to find work. The least she can do is help pay the tuition at that fancy private school. Kids today think they're entitled to everything. When I was her age, I was already working." Bob Miller was still speaking *sotto voce*.

Why the need for whispering? Lynn wondered, but she didn't want to raise his suspicions by seeming to be overly curious; she just wanted him to raise his voice a bit. Once she hit seventy, she noticed her hearing, along with her seeing and flatulence control, wasn't what it used to be. "Can you speak a little louder?"

"My hearing's gone to hell too. It's the shits to get old," Bob said in a slightly louder voice.

Lynn laughed politely. "What kind of work did you do, Bob? I hope you don't mind my calling you by your first name. You can call me Lynn."

"What else would I call ya?" Bob laughed and spit misted the air. "I worked in sales, have worked in sales all my life. I have a way with words, you know. Could sell an Eskimo a refrigerator." He laughed at his own joke, displaying particles of bread plastered to his unnaturally white teeth.

Lynn hoped the food was good because this promised to be a long lunch. When the waitress came to their table, she ordered a walnut, Gorgonzola, arugula salad and wild mushroom stuffed ravioli in a white wine sauce, plus a carafe of Chianti.

Lynn noticed Bob giving the girl the once over. *Embarrassing the things young women had to put up with.* To cover her discomfort, she asked for more bread. Bob ordered spaghetti and meatballs plus another martini. Since Bob promised to pay, Lynn was also prepared to order the *tiramisu* for dessert. She'd simply double her sit-ups tonight; she could do ten if she really tried.

While waiting for their food and beverages, Lynn got out her pillbox and took the tablets out for Friday. One by one, she swallowed the pills. She really didn't take this much medication normally, but she wanted to learn about Bob's medical problems and figured this might get him talking. So she "padded" her usual meds with some over the counter antacids. At least that was her intent.

Sometimes she got a little confused like the time she was disciplining her cat, intending to spray it gently with water and instead picked up the glass cleaner. The vet assured Lynn that Miss Kitty's blindness would be temporary. Or the time she gargled with Mr. Clean instead of Listerine. The liquids were the same color after all. As a multiple cat owner, she needed multiple bottles of Mr. Clean stored throughout her apartment to eradicate those nasty kitty "spills." Plus, she liked looking at Mr. Clean's muscular physique.

"Little lady, I didn't know you were a drug user," Bob said in an attempt at light conversation.

"These are just a few prescriptions to keep me young, you know. How about you, Bob? Do you have any prescription secrets to keep you young and virile?" Lynn asked in her little girl flirtatious way.

"Only a daily aspirin, you know for the old ticker. I've had some heart attack scares. I like to keep it simple. No need for any other meds, if you get my drift."

Apparently he wants me to know he can still get it up. What a disgusting thought.

"I certainly do, Bob," Lynn said as she took a huge gulp of the Chianti.

Just then a handsome gray-haired man in an impeccably tailored suit came to their table and gave Bob an envelope that he quickly put in his sports jacket pocket. "Thanks, Bob," he said as they shook hands.

Lynn stared unashamedly at the eye candy, unaware that she was doing exactly the same thing that Mr. Miller did to the waitress. *Eye Candy, mysterious envelope and Mr. Miller. Very interesting. There's more going on here than meets the eye.*

Just as Lynn was about to ask for an introduction, the waitress brought their food, but Lynn was so enamored with the delicious treats that she forgot to pursue her questioning. After a few mouthfuls of ravioli and a swig of Chianti, Lynn regained her focus.

"What a handsome, distinguished man. Who is he?"

"Just an old friend who owed me some money. I like to collect on my loans." Bob looked up and grinned, revealing more of his lunch.

They continued to make small talk until it came time for the check. When the waitress brought the check, Bob suddenly got up, wiped his face one more time, and said, "Thanks for the lunch, girlie. See ya back at the homestead." Lynn just looked at him in amazement as he exited the room. Her mother had always warned her about a free lunch.

Lynn wiped her mouth and then looked down to see a grease stain on her silk shell. "Ah shit," Lynn said, dipping her napkin in her water glass and rubbing at the stain, making it worse. "Dammit, looks like I've got a big dry cleaning bill ahead of me," she said as she took out her credit card and handed it to the waitress. The waitress just grinned, finding it slightly amusing that an old lady would swear.

Lynn left the restaurant with a feeling that Mr. Miller was doing something slightly offensive, but she just couldn't put her finger on it. Putting the receipt in her purse, she would continue to research Mr. Miller, the admitted cat killer and decidedly snarky salesman.

Meanwhile back at the homestead.

"Sweetums, mummy brought you some nummy ravioli," Lynn said to her five cats as she walked into her luxurious flat that smelled slightly of cat urine. She dished up the rich entree into five little bowls while the cats brushed against her ankles. "I don't know what's wrong with Mummy. Suddenly Mummy is very, very sleepy." Lynn yawned as she went to her bedroom to sleep off the two Tylenol P.M. she had taken by mistake and the two glasses of Chianti she had drunk on purpose.

CHAPTER 3

Priests and their Peccadilloes

"Bless us, Father, for we have sinned," Margaret said into her cell phone. There was a long pause and then a booming laugh.

"Margaret, I've missed you. How've you been?" Father Patrick Mallory, dean of students at the University of St. Mark's, leaned back in his chair and cradled the phone against his cheek. Patrick Mallory was over six feet tall and trim with white thick, curly hair. He could still turn female heads, no doubt some males as well.

"I've missed you too, Patrick. I need to talk with you— talk only, Patrick."

"Ah, to recapture our youth. Wouldn't that be lovely? I have such fond memories of our little trysts in college."

"Then you had to dump me for the priesthood. I never quite forgave you for that."

"That wasn't what it seemed when we went out to dinner a few years ago. You seemed quite eager to forgive me."

"Don't you try to sweet talk me. Remember I know you well."

"That you do, my dear. So what do I owe this honor?"

"I would like to meet Father Flynn."

"And why would a lovely lady like yourself want to meet a rascal like Flynn?"

"I'm doing a little research on priests and their peccadilloes."

"I hope I'm not on your list."

"You can relax, Patrick. I wouldn't advertise your indiscretions because it would be totally hypocritical and, as you know, I'm not a hypocrite."

"That you're not, Margaret. But I do remember a gullible young Catholic who started an organization called COME." Patrick started to chuckle.

"Don't bring that up again. I just wanted to initiate some social activism: Catholics on the Move for Equality. It was a noble effort."

"It would have been if everybody hadn't been laughing so hard. Oh, the 'come' jokes that flew around campus every time you held a rally. My favorite was 'Oh come all ye Faithful.' I still can't hear that Christmas carol without laughing. Believe me, I've gotten in trouble a few times over your political efforts."

"You've gotten into trouble over a lot of things, Patrick, but enough of our college memories. Let's get back to Father Flynn."

"Your call, Margaret. I'm rather sad you've lost that charming gullibility."

"I've lost lots of my college innocence, especially when it comes to the church. That's one of the reasons I want to research Father Flynn's indiscretions."

"I believe the word you used earlier was peccadilloes. I'd hardly call embezzling over $25,000 from the parish a peccadillo; however, several of his young male parishioners have complained of sexual improprieties that might fall under that category. Father Flynn has been advised to keep mum about the allegations, so I'm not sure you'll get much information. Are you finally getting around to that book you've always wanted to write?"

"It's a delicate matter, Patrick, but I'm working with some friends on a little project that's highly confidential."

"I don't suppose you'd confess what's really going on. I'd have to keep confidentiality, you know."

"I'm not really interested in confession at this point, my dear. Maybe later," Margaret said, laughing.

"What would you like from me, Margaret? Other than the usual."

"I'm getting too old for the 'usual,' Patrick."

"Never, my dear."

"You never change, always the charming, but dirty, old man."

"It's an acquired skill, Margaret."

"The dirt or the charm?"

"Both I must admit."

"I'd simply like to know how to reach Father Flynn. I want to get a feel for him." Father Mallory laughed.

"You know I didn't mean it like that, Patrick. I want to know what kind of man he is. Remember when we'd use the word *vibe*? I'd like to see what kind of vibes the man gives off."

"You always were a good judge of *vibes*. I'd like to get your take on Peter once you do meet him. He often goes to the campus coffee shop right after morning mass at St. Mark's chapel. Sometimes students join him, but most of the time he's by himself. You could just happen to be there tomorrow after mass, say around noon. Maybe you could stop by my office after your little conversation. How does that sound?"

"That sounds lovely, Patrick, but no hanky-panky."

"We'll see. I'll have a bottle of your favorite Chardonnay on ice, just in case you change your mind."

"You are incorrigible," Margaret said, laughing. "See you tomorrow." Margaret couldn't continue the conversation because she had an appointment for a massage with Carlos followed by a manicure and pedicure in the deluxe in-house spa. And then there was the bloody doctor.

* * *

After a somewhat restless night, Margaret decided to get up early and do a brief work out with her personal trainer.

Then she showered and chose a wig she knew Patrick would like. Even though their affair had been over for some time, she still felt the need to impress her former lover. Since her legs and her breasts were her best features, she'd decided to wear that fashionably short, clingy sage green silk sheath with her favorite high-heeled sandals. She might even weaken and have a glass of that lovely French Chardonnay. The beautiful summer day had romantic potential indeed. *What am I thinking?* Margaret knew exactly what she was thinking. While others felt guilty thinking "impure" thoughts, Margaret felt renewed energy and youthful optimism. It was her cross to bear. She was a far cry from the girl who organized COME.

A lapsed Catholic, Margaret passed on the mass and instead went straight to the coffee shop to wait for Father Flynn. She recognized him immediately even though he had grown a beard, no doubt to hide his "weak chin." His picture didn't do him justice. He was far handsomer than the black and white photo she had found on the Internet.

Just as Patrick had predicted, he was sitting alone in a reading chair against the wall underneath the Fighting Marksmen mural. You'd think they'd change the mural after St. Mark's became co-ed. *Some things never change. Men just can't relinquish their power and need to control, to say nothing of their need for attention and adoration.* Margaret, in spite of years of therapy, resisted self-analysis, or she would have realized that description also fit her. Apart from a few students the coffee shop was nearly empty.

After studying Father Flynn for several minutes, Margaret got up from her chair and went to initiate a conversation. "Excuse me, Father, may I have a word?"

When she got closer she could see that Father Flynn looked older than his seventy years and very tired. The negative publicity had definitely taken its toll. Still, he was gracious to Margaret as he invited her to join him.

"What can I do for you?"

"I'm not exactly sure how to explain."

"You could start by introducing yourself."

"Of course, how silly of me. My name is Margaret."

"Does Margaret have a last name?"

"It's Thompson. Forgive me. I'm a bit nervous." She held out her hand. Reluctantly, Father Flynn shook Margaret's hand. Margaret had had better handshakes from the golden retriever the official high-rise dog walker walked daily.

Margaret paused and fiddled with her cultured pearl necklace. Then she looked directly into Father Flynn's intense brown eyes.

"Would you like some coffee or tea?" Father Peter Flynn returned Margaret's stare.

"No thank you." Margaret finally broke eye contact and looked at her hands folded on her lap. Even as a kid she had lost staring contests.

"I suspect you know about the accusations against me."

Margaret was clearly uncomfortable. She stammered, twiddled her pearls, and twisted her long, blonde, fake pageboy. After a very long pause, she nodded her head.

"I think that's exactly why I want to talk to you. I wondered how your faith was holding up." She almost felt sorry for him.

"I've been advised by my attorneys not to comment, but I'd be happy to talk about your faith."

"I'll take that cup of tea now," Margaret said. Father Flynn motioned to a young man behind the counter to bring two cups of tea to his table.

Margaret and Peter Flynn talked about an hour while sipping their tea. They talked about what it meant to be a Christian in a corrupt world. They got into a general discussion about good and evil, faith, an afterlife, always keeping the conversation impersonal. This was more a theological discussion between student and professor than an honest, personal dialogue. She found him intelligent and somewhat depressed, but confident in basic Catholic doctrine. The Pope was still infallible; birth control, gay marriage, and abortion were wrong; and the priesthood was reserved for celibate men. No women allowed in the good old boys' Catholic club.

"Thank you for your time, Father." Margaret left the interview feeling a bit disappointed in herself, like she had studied for a big test and then couldn't remember any of the information.

When she went to see Patrick in his office after her disturbingly nonproductive discussion with Father Flynn, she was ready for a glass of wine. Patrick was just the man for the job. After a brief hug and a chaste kiss on the cheek, Patrick ushered her to a comfortable leather chair while he sat on the couch.

"Well, Margaret, how did you find Peter Flynn?" Patrick put his feet up on the coffee table.

"I wasn't as disgusted as I was expecting to be, and you were right: I got no information about the allegations. However, we did have a predictable conversation about the mysteries of life and death. You don't have to worry about Father Flynn rocking the Catholic boat. He is more conservative than Ted Cruz."

Patrick laughed. "Except for that little embezzlement issue."

"There is that. I'm curious why you don't seem all that upset about the sexual allegations. The money seems more important to you."

"Unlike you, Margaret, I am a hypocrite. Let's just leave it at that, shall we?" Patrick went to the ice bucket and poured them both a glass of chardonnay. "Still contemplating the Big Cosmic Questions, even after all these years. I would have thought that with your life experiences you would have let some of that go." He handed her the wine.

"Such irony, Patrick. You're the religious one and I'm the lapsed one, yet you are comfortable with your quick, glib answers to some very difficult questions. And I, I am still trying to figure things out. I just can't help it."

"Margaret, what is really going on with you? You don't seem your usual upbeat self."

"It's a long story, but I don't think I'm quite up to sharing it right now. Let's just say that I'm embarking on a very interesting journey."

"I love a woman of mystery. Here's to your journey, my dear." Patrick held up his glass and toasted his former lover.

"Patrick, if you don't mind, I would just like to sit next to you with your arm around my shoulders. Nothing more."

"Always happy to oblige, Margaret." Patrick started to hum: "'Come together, right now, over you.'"

"Don't start with me, old man," Margaret said as she gently punched his shoulder. Margaret, a strong, self-sufficient, albeit vain woman, allowed herself to be held by a very dear, if hypocritical, friend.

CHAPTER 4

And the Winner Is...

"Ladies, ladies, I'm trying to call this Friday's meeting to order." Margaret raised her voice and her glass, only to be ignored by her three friends who were arguing about their nominees. Once again she took her sterling silver iced-tea spoon and gently rapped on the crystal. Finally she had their attention.

"Let's do this systematically, nominee by nominee. We'll follow the order of the nominations. Tell us what you've discovered on your own and then we'll go to Susan for her in depth Internet research. Susan, I believe you were the first. What did you dig up on Henry Beckler?"

"What you've read in the paper is public knowledge: the millions squandered, the wives and mistresses, the bankruptcy that infuriated his creditors, the DUIs.

But I dug a little deeper and found out a few interesting tidbits from his past. First of all, he came from humble beginnings. His parents were farmers outside of Clearwater, close to St. Cloud. Henry, an only child, went to high school in St. Cloud where he excelled in absolutely nothing except good looks. I must say he was one hunky looking guy with a killer grin and dimples, cheeks and chin. I'm a sucker for dimples. I was a big Tom Sellick fan until I found out he was a NRA freak."

"Easy girl," Karen said with a grin that showed her dimples.

"I thought you said your info was 'interesting.' Not so far, girlfriend. Let's hear the juicy shit," Lynn said, wiping peach juice from her chin.

"Wait for it." Susan paused. The dames gave her their full attention.

"After graduating, he went into the Army and was dishonorably discharged."

"Now we're getting there. What did Mr. Beckler do?" Lynn asked. The others nodded enthusiastically.

"While drunk on leave, he sexually assaulted a woman." The women gasped collectively.

"He was subsequently court-marshaled and served a brief military prison term before he was dishonorably discharged."

"Serves him right," Margaret added. "Please continue, Susan."

"After he was discharged, he went back to St. Cloud and knocked up a local girl who happened to have some family money, married her and convinced her to invest in a small auto dealership in St. Cloud. Henry was a born salesman and made a good living selling new and used cars. When his wife discovered his mistress, she divorced him and 'took him to the cleaners.' Then came wife number two, another woman with some money."

"I don't get it. Why would a rich woman, or any woman, for that matter, even consider such a sleazebag?" Karen asked, almost missing a stitch on that precious afghan of hers.

"You forget the dimples and the killer grin," Susan said.

"I heard that men with dimples have big penises or is it the size of their thumbs? I forget," Lynn said.

"I heard it was the size of their feet, though that couldn't be true because my second husband had huge feet and the tiniest, well you know," Karen said, not missing a stitch.

"Girls, focus. Susan, what else? We need to move on," Margaret said, trying to maintain a modicum of control, though mentally she was taking inventory of previous husbands' and lovers' feet and thumbs since none of them had dimples.

"With the help of wife number two, he kept his business and it thrived. Then his parents died and left him the farm, which he sold at an enormous profit. With all that discretionary income, Henry got 'too big for his britches,' as my grandma used to say. He started to play the big shot, buying a fancy house bordering the St. Cloud Country Club and a condo in the Cities for 'entertainment' purposes."

"And we all know what kind of 'entertainment' Henry preferred," Margaret said.

"As you can imagine, wife number two divorced him as well. Now Mr. Beckler is on the brink of financial ruin. Rumor has it that he is hiding in Sante Fe where he owns yet another condo, at least until the bankruptcy is settled."

"Anything else of interest, Susan?"

"I was saving the best for last. Apparently Mr. Beckler is pyrophobic. He has an extreme fear of fire, specifically campfires or fireplaces. Can you believe that none of his homes had fireplaces? I couldn't get through the winter without my fireplace." The Dames nodded in agreement.

"What's the story on the phobia?" Lynn asked.

"When he was around four years old, he burned himself while roasting marshmallows. He wears long sleeved shirts exclusively to cover the scars."

"Poor baby," Lynn said. "How can we plan to hurt someone who has been so terribly hurt himself? He's like the last cat I rescued who had been abused. I can't possibly vote for him."

"Imagine no more s-mores," Karen said, laughing at her semi-clever word play.

"No need to make up your mind quite yet, Lynn. We still have three potential clients to review. And you're next, Lynn."

"As you all know, I nominated our very own neighbor, Mr. Bob Miller, who bragged to me about running down a cat with his fancy car." The Dames made noises in mock horror.

"Mock me if you will, but I guarantee you won't be mocking me when I tell you what I've discovered. As you know, I agreed to meet Mr. Miller for lunch to get to know him better and I certainly did. He had horrible manners and food on his fake white teeth. It was disgusting. To top things off, he gave the check to me! How cheap is that?"

"Now that is an 'extermination' just waiting to happen," Karen said sarcastically.

"Just wait, Karen. During lunch some very mysterious things occurred. Shortly after we were seated, the owner of the restaurant, Marco Costello, came to our table and whispered loud enough for me to hear, 'Send her by around three tomorrow afternoon.'"

"How did Mr. Miller explain the comment?" Margaret asked.

"He said it was for his grand niece who was interviewing for a job in the deli."

"That doesn't seem out of line to me," Margaret said.

"But why all the whispering?"

"Maybe he didn't want to share personal information with the other diners, like a lot of people do while talking on their cell phones," Margaret said. "I can respect someone with boundaries."

"Here's the next weird thing. In the middle of my wild mushroom ravioli, which was absolutely delicious, by the way, a very distinguished, well-dressed man slipped Bob an envelope that was apparently full of cash. He also whispered."

"There it is, girls: death to whisperers!" Karen said. As the Dames laughed, Lynn desperately looked around the room for some support. Just then Susan looked up from the flourless chocolate torte she was focused on.

"Lynn is right. Mr. Miller might not be what he seems. He might be much more than a cat killer."

"Thank you, Susan." Lynn looked around the room. If she had been five years old, she would have said, "So there" and stuck out her tongue.

Instead she said, "I just knew that he was up to no good. 'Boundaries,' my ass." And then stuck out her tongue for emphasis.

"I've found out that a Bob (aka Bobby Big Boy Miller), about the same age as our neighbor, has served time for promoting prostitution."

"I wonder how big his thumbs or feet are," Karen said as she slipped the needles in and out.

"You are so bad, Decrease," Lynn said with a grin.

"He also made his money in sales, including the sale of young women. If, and if is the operative word here, the Bob Millers are one and the same, the whispered comments make sense. It sounds to me like he's still an operator."

"You mean I had lunch with a pimp?" Lynn looked horrified.

"It means you *may* have had lunch with a pimp. We still need to verify if our Bob Miller is the same as the object of my research."

"Any more surprises, Susan?"

"No. The other two candidates were pretty much as described in our previous meeting unless Karen or Margaret got additional information."

Karen shook her head. "I was hoping you'd find more info on the porno-loving custodian. I could just see him with a broom handle up his ... oops, almost lost a stitch."

Margaret interrupted before Karen got too graphic and summarized her "interview" with Father Peter Flynn, the "fiddler," omitting her meeting with Patrick.

When Margaret was done, Susan said, "If we vote for either the custodian or the priest, I'll try to dig deeper. I got a bit involved with researching Henry and Bob Miller and neglected the other candidates."

"Well, Dames, if no one objects..." Margaret looked around the room. No one objected. "I believe it's time to vote. I'll try to summarize. There's Henry Becker, the philandering sexual predator who's hiding in Sante Fe. Next is Mr. Bob Miller, a possible pimp living in our own high rise. Our pedophile custodian is in jail awaiting trial. And Father Peter Flynn is waiting trial for embezzlement right here in St. Paul."

"It looks to me like it's down to two: Bob Miller and Peter Flynn. They're the only two we would have access to," Susan said.

"And, to tell the truth, after I met Father Flynn last Saturday after mass, I had nothing but sympathy for him. He seemed a lost soul and very remorseful.

Even though his attorneys forbade him to comment, I did get some feelings from the man. I'm not sure I could live with 'exterminating' a priest," Margaret added.

"You always did have a soft spot for priests," Karen said as she patted Margaret's hand. On one of the Dames' weekends away, Margaret had confessed her liaisons with Patrick Mallory.

"It's time, Dames."

Margaret handed out the blank sheets of paper and kept one for herself. After a few seconds, she collected the ballots and quickly read them. "And our new client is … drum roll please." The Dames pounded on whatever hard surface was nearby.

"Bob Miller!"

The Dames cheered and raised their glasses.

"I just knew it. Diet be damned. I'm celebrating!" Lynn said as she had her second piece of cake.

"Before we get too far into the planning, we need to make sure our Mr. Miller is in fact a practicing pimp. There are many Bob Millers out there. Let's make sure we get the right one. We'll need more personal info on Miller: family, siblings, age, birthplace, education, anything to nail down his identity.

Lynn, do you have any idea who the second gentleman was, the one who slipped Mr. Miller the cash? We can research the restaurant's owner pretty easily I think, but we really need to nail down the other man before we make specific 'extermination' plans." Susan had slipped into full investigator mode.

"I'll make another luncheon date and see what info I can get," Lynn said. "I'll have the ravioli again because it was absolutely delish. Maybe a different salad. I saw a very pretty Caesar with shrimp delivered to the next table." Lynn was off and running, the girls laughing at their dear friend. Lynn was famous for her *non sequiturs*, so much so that the Dames gave her a t-shirt that said, "What don't you understand about ADD. Look there's a chicken." Lynn looked around puzzled at their laughter.

"If all goes well, maybe I'll get an invite to his apartment. Then I could snoop around, maybe check out family photos." Lynn regained her focus, at least for the moment.

"Right, you research his family: sibs, wives, children, etc.," Susan said.

"Just be careful he doesn't try anything. Once he gets you into his lair, who knows? He might recruit you for his elderly clients," Karen said with a grin.

"Now if I were Margaret, I could see your point," Lynn said. When it came to sexual matters, Lynn had no confidence at all. Ever since her husband had made plans to run off with the receptionist bimbo, she had felt overweight and unattractive. A pass from the snarky Mr. Miller just might do great things for her self-confidence. Or not. Mr. Miller wasn't exactly a hot geezer.

Susan looked at Margaret with a gleam in her eye. *It might come to that. Margaret was one sexy lady. She was the Closer, after all.*

"I can make a visit to his apartment on the pretense of Association business since I'm on the Board. We do have that landscape issue on the agenda," Margaret said, sensing she was needed. "I could make my pitch about needing to update our plantings by adding perennial gardens and replacing those dying flowering crab apple trees. If I can get into his apartment, I can snoop around as well."

"If he offers you something to drink, take it and then ask to use the restroom. You can find out tons of stuff by looking in medicine cabinets," Susan suggested. That's how she discovered a few of Margaret's "beauty" secrets.

Because Susan's wheelchair didn't fit into the guest's half bath, Susan had to use Margaret's huge master bath. Susan discovered Margaret was spending a small fortune on anti-wrinkle creams tastefully displayed in hand blown glass. And she also had an ample supply of much less expensive sexual lubricants stashed away in vanity drawers. Oh, yes, and the bottle of Astroglide on the counter that Susan almost used as hand sanitizer.

Margaret looked twenty years younger than her actual age which the Dames thought was probably due to the sex as much as the beauty products. The Dames were unaware that Margaret staged her bathroom for their benefit. It was her little joke.

In addition to the sexual lubricants, Susan found pills, lots and lots of pills. She could never remember the names of all the drugs, so the next time she needed to use the loo she brought in a pen and some paper in her pants pocket. Unfortunately, there was no need because all of the pills had disappeared. Susan bemoaned the fact that her disability prevented her from tackling the medicine cabinet. All those meds, very odd indeed. Susan was truly puzzled because her beloved friend could not be an addict or a dealer. Both were totally out of character.

"Good idea. We all have our assignments, all except you, Karen. Any ideas?"

"I could always knit something for the old guy, maybe a hat or lap robe?"

"And why would you do that? You don't even know him," Lynn said.

"Good point. I'm sick of knitting for people who don't appreciate the time and expense it takes to knit. Dumb idea. Any suggestions?"

"You could have lunch the same day Lynn and Mr. Miller have their second 'date' and just watch to see if the handsome, unidentified gentleman shows up. Then ask around. Maybe the wait staff or bartender would know. He's probably a regular."

"Good idea, better than knitting something. Now I just need a description of the gentleman. This sounds like fun. I do love their ravioli," Karen said, satisfied she was doing something useful.

"I'll research Marco Costello, restaurant and deli owner," Susan volunteered. "Once we find out the name of the mystery gent, I'll tackle him as well."

"Right. We all have our assignments. So to summarize: Lynn, lunch and family snooping; Karen, lunch and mysterious gentleman identification; Susan, Marco Costello and mystery man research, and finally scintillating, challenging potty patrol for me. Until next week, ladies, onward and upward. Or should I say downward."

"No whining allowed, Margaret. It's only the very best who get assigned loo-looky-looky."

"Looky me," Margaret said, laughing.

CHAPTER 5

Miller 101

Mid-morning the next day, Margaret called Mr. Miller, alleged pimp, to arrange an appointment to discuss Association business. He gave her the business instead.

"What Association business is so damn important we need to meet face-to-face? I'm a busy man, girlie." *I hate when you call me girlie.*

Margaret took a deep breath and a sip of her hot tea before she answered. "Each Board member was assigned five home owners to visit and you were assigned to me. We want to show you our proposal for the garden and landscape update. You know we have some flowering crabs that need replacement."

"You're confusin' me with someone who gives a shit."

Talk about a crab without the flowers. This extermination will be a pleasure. Margaret felt like she was a character in *A Christmas Carol* asking Mr. Scrooge for a charitable donation. "Please, Mr. Miller, it will only take a few minutes. We do value your input."

"Do you bake?"

"Excuse me?" Margaret was having a hard time tracking the old guy. A *non sequitur* worthy of Lynn.

"Pretty straight forward if you ask me. Do you bake? I might be persuaded to talk with you if you brought some cookies or somethin'. My wife used to bake the best lemon bars. No chocolate though. I'm allergic. No nuts either."

Margaret had to bite her tongue. *No nuts indeed.*

"I'm sure I can manage some lemon bars, Mr. Miller. What time would be convenient for you?"

"I'll see you at nine tomorrow morning. I have an appointment later in the morning so make it snappy and don't forget those lemon bars, though I doubt yours will equal Edith's, may she rest in peace." He sighed then hung up the phone.

What Margaret wouldn't do for love and death. Margaret took a note card from her desk and wrote:

Allergic to chocolate and nuts; dead wife's name is Edith. Likes lemon bars. Is rude and swears. Called me girlie. A little ADD. Not interested in Association business. She filed the note card and went to get herself ready for her personal trainer. Then it was lunch at the Lexington, her favorite.

* * *

Lynn had called Mr. Miller right after the Dames' last meeting. They were scheduled for a luncheon date the next day at eleven. Karen would also be there watching and waiting for the mysterious, well-dressed hottie to appear. Because Karen was a major frump, Margaret took her aside and gave her some wardrobe advice. This was no time for too small hand-knit sweaters.

Mr. Miller wondered about his increasing popularity. First, it was that dumpy woman, who inhaled her lunch, asking for a second date, then Margaret something or other asking to meet about Association business. His wife, Edith, used to say that men just got more attractive as they age and women just got gray, fat, and downright ugly. He might as well relax and enjoy the female attention ... and the lemon bars. Edith might just have been right. He had noticed younger women giving him the eye. And who could blame them? He was an attractive older man of means after all. Why wouldn't they be interested?

Exactly at nine, Mr. Miller, all buffed and polished, answered the door to find an attractive blonde woman in a peach colored A-line shift carrying a covered plate of lemon bars and a small leather bag. It was his lucky day.

"I come bearing gifts," Margaret said when Mr. Miller opened the door. Margaret walked into a luxury suite that was decorated with large upholstered pieces covered in chintz prints, lace curtains on all the windows, silk flower arrangements, fake plants, and exceptionally ugly figurines of dogs and shepherdesses. Between the cranberry peony flowered wallpaper and the chintz, Margaret felt like she was in Laura Ashley hell. The dining room table with its lace tablecloth was covered with Bob's breakfast dishes. Margaret hadn't seen such bad taste since she was a child visiting her grandparents in St. Paul.

"You'll have to excuse the mess. The maid doesn't come in until later today," Bob said, obviously uncomfortable with the breakfast clutter.

"No problem. Just let me get the landscape plans and I'll get right to it," Margaret said, reaching into her leather bag.

"Would you like some coffee, tea ... or me?" Mr. Miller chuckled.

Margaret's first impulse was to quickly excuse herself, but then she remembered her "loo looky-looky" duty.

"Thanks, that would be lovely, the tea, that is."

While Mr. Miller went into the kitchen, Margaret took a much closer look at the clutter surrounding her, looking specifically for family photos. She wandered to the bookcase to check out a series of pictures of beautiful young women all with thick, long hair and heavy makeup. They couldn't all be grandchildren.

"Checking out my beauties, I see," Mr. Miller said as he set a tea tray on the dining room table. Margaret did admire the Spode china, the only thing she did admire.

"Tell me about them. Are they family members?"

"Not exactly. These dolls are my extended family. You see I mentor young women who need career guidance. I guide them to very fulfilling careers."

41

I bet you do. Margaret took a picture off the shelf. "Tell me about this young woman."

"Ah, you picked one of my favorites. This sweetie came to me when she was sixteen. Her family had kicked her out because they couldn't control her; she was skipping school and had started drinking heavily and smoking pot. I heard about her from one of my old frat brothers and invited her to stay with Edith and me. Once she moved in with us, she turned herself around. She got her GED and went on to become a cosmetologist. Tiffany is one of my bigger success stories."

"You must be very proud. I had no idea you were into such acts of charity."

"I don't consider these girls charity. They have to work hard for all I give 'em. Now let me pour you some tea. Some lemon bars?"

"You're most kind." Margaret politely made small talk and drank two cups of very weak herbal mint tea. By the time she explained the landscape plans, she really did need to use the restroom.

"May I use your ladies' room, Mr. Miller? I still have three more homeowners to see this morning." Mr. Miller pointed to the hallway leading to the bedrooms. Glancing into a bedroom wallpapered with humongous hydrangeas, she saw a white lace canopied bed. Suddenly she felt very sorry for Tiffany and the other girls who had to endure such exaggerated femininity. And how could Mr. Miller survive such massive doses of estrogen? She reminded herself to check on the circumstances of Edith's death.

She finally found the guest bath, pink flowers on the walls, the towels, even the rug. No surprise there. She would have only a few minutes to search, thank god. She was beginning to get a serious headache from floral overdose. Starting with the medicine cabinet she checked for prescription and nonprescription drugs. There were the usual aspirin bottles and hand-lotions, but nothing of note to indicate any meds

Bob might be taking. She did, however, find a wheel of what looked like birth control pills. Curious. She didn't realize that Mr. Miller still had a young guest. After flushing the pink toilet, she washed her hands with the pink soap and dried them on the rose covered towel. *Thank God, I can get out of here. I will never look at flowers in the same way again.*

Margaret gathered her things and thanked him for the tea. As she was moving toward the door, Bob stopped her and asked, "Can I have a hug?" He grinned, showing his unnaturally white pointed teeth that seemed slightly feral. *He's really getting to me.*

"Excuse me?" Margaret laughed nervously and sidestepped her neighbor. *Creepy, creepy, creepy.*

"Okay, I get that you're a little shy. Maybe next time."

In your dreams. Just the thought made her shiver.

"Thanks again for the tea. May I count on your support for the landscape plans?"

"If I get that hug," Mr. Miller leered.

"Maybe next time."

As she walked to the elevator, her breathing slowed and she could feel her blood pressure return to normal. When she opened the door to her apartment she sighed, looked around, and thanked god no chintz, lace, flowered wallpaper, or dirty old men greeted her.

She went to her desk, took out her note cards and added:

Miller as "mentor" to young women. Pictures of over a dozen young women who all looked somewhat similar: big hair and heavy makeup. Tiffany lived with him and Edith. He considers her one of his big "successes." Found what looked to be birth control pills in guest bath. Has a maid (maybe one of his "dolls?"). Likes lemon bars and drinks herbal tea. Wife had unbelievably bad decorating taste. Find out how she died. Creepy old sleaze wanted hugs.

CHAPTER 6

"Let's do lunch."

Karen arrived at the Italian restaurant a bit earlier than Lynn and Mr. Miller. She wore a tan linen pants suit with a lacy hand knit rust shawl, both wardrobe suggestions from Margaret, her self-appointed wardrobe consultant. This particular shawl, one of her best efforts, was a State Fair prizewinner.

Since she was alone, she sat at the bar which would give her access to the restaurant and the bartender who probably knew the regulars.

She was sipping a glass of chilled *Sauvignon blanc* when she saw the *maitre'd* seat Lynn and Mr. Miller at a table for two facing the river. All she had to do was watch for a distinguished, impeccably dressed gray-haired man and find out his identity. And stay sober. It was hard to predict which task would be more difficult. Karen wasn't famous for holding her liquor and it was still morning after all. She had also skimped on breakfast, not a good thing.

Unfortunately, there were already three distinguished elderly gentlemen fitting Lynn's sketchy description seated together. Now if only one of these gentlemen would go over to talk with Mr. Miller, she could ask Vince, the bartender, to identify him.

Just then Vince asked her if she would like another glass of wine.

"Certainement," Karen said with a grin. Everyone knew that when Karen started tossing out French expressions, she was already feeling her wine. When Karen was married to hubby number two, she traveled to France on her honeymoon. Karen felt that two years of high school French and a honeymoon in Paris entitled her to speak the occasional French. *C'est dommage.*

When the waiter brought her the wine and a complimentary bread basket, she ordered the wild mushroom ravioli. She looked at Vince, batted what few eyelashes remained and said, "It comes highly recommended."

"Excellent choice." Vince, no doubt used to old broads' flirtations, didn't bat an eye or an eyelash.

By the time her entree arrived, Karen was feeling no pain. *What the hell, I might as well ask him to identify all three of the hotties.*

"Could you tell me the name of the three gentlemen sitting over there, *s'il vous plait*?" She pointed at the table and in the process nearly fell off the bar stool. The distinguished older gentleman sitting next to her grabbed her elbow and prevented the embarrassing fall. Karen regained her composure and looked into the most beautiful face. *Mon Dieu, it's an elderly George Clooney.*

"Merci, monsieur," Karen giggled. "My medications make me dizzy, especially when I drink wine."

"I understand. Perhaps I can answer your question. Allow me to introduce myself. George Clark at your service." *George Clark, George Clooney, close enough.*

"You've already been most helpful. I was just wondering who those gentlemen were. They seem to be enjoying themselves."

"That they are. They're old friends who meet here once a week to discuss politics, the stock market, and other mutual interests. I was just on my way to join them; we were in the same fraternity at the U. Go Gophers." George grinned, a dimple in each cheek. "I'd better join them before they give up on me. It was a pleasure meeting you." He smiled displaying perfect teeth.

Dimples, does that mean? Karen remembered Lynn's comments about dimples and penis size. *And perfect teeth.* Sacre bleu. *Whatever happened to imperfect teeth?* Karen smiled back and then dabbed her lips with her napkin, hiding her slight overbite. Then she dug into her warm ravioli and it was delicious, though not as delicious as George Clark. It was after about three bites that she realized she still didn't know the men's names.

* * *

"Nice to see you again, Bob. I so enjoyed our last lunch."

"Likewise." Just then Johnny Cash started to sing "Folsom Prison Blues." Bob fumbled for his phone, got out of his chair, and quickly walked to the foyer without so much as a "Sorry" or "Excuse me." Lynn almost left in disgust, but knew she had to get more info on the sleaze. She ordered a glass of the house red to keep her company.

While she was waiting for her beverage, she noticed Karen talking to The Man. She tried getting her attention, but that was impossible because she was so totally enthralled with him. She needed to get her attention somehow—a note would work. She found an old business card from her insurance agent and wrote on the back: "He's the one! Get his name." When her waiter brought her wine, she asked him to deliver the note. She watched as Karen turned and gave a thumb's up. Mission accomplished.

Karen's accomplishment helped mollify Lynn's anger. The wine also helped.

"Any chance that we can talk?" Lynn asked once Bob returned.

"What do you want to talk about?" Bob asked. "I'm not one of those metrosexual guys who has manicures and talks about his feelings."

"No surprise there," Lynn mumbled, knowing that Bob was hard of hearing. "I was hoping that I could get to know you better?"

"Not a chance, girlie. I'm not attracted to older women. Edith used to say men just get more attractive and women well ... they just get ugly."

"Excuse me? Just who do you think you are? If you think I was suggesting anything romantic, you're even more of an ass than I thought."

"Give it a rest, girlie. I came here to eat and that's what I intend to do, with you or without you."

"Spaghetti with meat balls, I imagine. Try not to spill. Young girls don't like old geezers who need bibs." She picked up her wine and tossed the last few sips onto Bob's sports coat. "Oops, the wine's on you. Literally," Lynn said as she threw her napkin on the table. Bob just looked at her and sputtered.

She walked directly to the bar to pick up Karen. When she looked back, Bob was sponging off his coat. Then he moved to the all male table where much laughter ensued.

"Come on, Karen, I'll take you home. You're in no condition to drive. We can pick up your car tonight. I can't believe you got shit-faced on two glasses of wine."

"Three glasses. George bought me a drink," she slurred. "You're right: He is the one. Can we stop at that cute little yarn shop, Pull the Wool Over Your Eyes. I need to go to my happy place."

"I think you're already there, hon."

CHAPTER 7

Plotting his demise

Margaret was ready for the Dames: iced tea, a lemon meringue pie from her favorite bakery, her note cards, and her white board and markers. Mr. Miller's lemon bars had inspired her pie choice as had Mr. Miller. Margaret could imagine her satisfaction rubbing that pie in his creepy, smarmy face. Just seeing that white board got her creative juices flowing. The women filed in ready for the brainstorming session.

"Dames, it's time to report on all you've found out about Mr. Miller et al. When we get all the info we can discuss possible means for the extermination."

"That's the fun part," Lynn said. "I love coming up with a variety of scenarios, especially now that we've decided Mr. Miller is our new client. Planning the demise of the world's biggest asshole should be a blast."

"I couldn't agree more," Karen said.

"I don't mean to be rude or anything, but you were too sloshed and too enamored with George, the dimpled darling, to notice Mr. Miller's assholiness," Lynn said, trying to keep things real.

"'Assholiness?' You've got to be kidding me," Margaret said, laughing. "You certainly have a way with words. It sounds like you're addressing the last Pope. I shudder to think what we'd have to kiss, certainly not his ring."

"Thank you, Margaret, for that image."

"You're welcome. Okay, who wants to start?" The Dames valued their manners after all.

Susan nodded. "I'll start with the info on Marco Costello, the restaurant and deli owner. Mr. Costello was picked up on a 'John' sting back a few years ago. His lawyers got him off by pleading entrapment. Oh, and he had a DUI five years before that. I also found out that he had four financial backers for his restaurant, one of whom is our Bob Miller."

"Any chance one of the others might be George Clark?" Karen asked.

"How did you know?"

"I'll bring you up to speed when it's my turn," Karen said.

"I wonder where Miller got his money," Margaret said. "When I visited his condo, I was shocked by the ugly furnishings and decorating."

"Just because you have money doesn't guarantee good taste," Lynn volunteered.

"No kidding. The Millers' condo could win an award for kitsch. It was like the decorator had the flower flu and regurgitated posies all over the walls and the furniture. He deserves extermination just for that."

"The decorator or Mr. Miller?" Karen said with a grin.

"Both, in my opinion," Margaret said.

"Maybe his deceased wife left him a bundle. I'll get right on it," Susan said as she clicked away on her laptop.

"Any more relevant info on Costello, Susan?" Margaret asked. Susan stopped and shook her head.

"Karen, what do you have to report?"

"After I finished my wardrobe consult," Karen smiled at Margaret, "I drove to the restaurant and had a glass of wine to relax myself."

"She was very relaxed," Lynn whispered to no one in particular.

"When Lynn and Mr. Miller arrived, I sort of got sidetracked."

"That's an understatement," Lynn said. "She got snockered and then nearly fell off her bar stool when Mr. Handsome, Karen's own superhero, rescued her."

"As much as I hate to admit it, Lynn is right. I was a bit tipsy, but I did complete my assignment:

I identified the mysterious stranger slash superhero. His name is George Clark and he's a friend with three other guys who all graduated from the U and were in the same fraternity. They meet regularly to discuss politics, the stock market, and Lord knows what else. Bob Miller joined them right after Lynn dumped her wine on him."

Both Susan and Margaret gasped. "I would have loved to have seen that," Margaret said.

"I was brilliant, if I do say so myself."

Karen continued, "They're probably all in cahoots. So what do we do if that's the case? We can't exterminate them all."

"Just one extermination at a time, Dames. We need to keep our focus." Margaret pulled the group together. Just then Susan interrupted.

"Info update. Here's the skinny on Edith Miller. Bob was Edith's second husband; her first was a wealthy stock broker who died leaving her with a substantial inheritance. So that's probably where Bob got his cash. But why would Edith allow Bob to bring in young women to 'mentor'? Couldn't she see that he was up to no good?"

"Love is blind, deaf, and dumb, Susan," Karen said.

"That reminds me Bob is also hard of hearing," Lynn said. "I didn't want to forget that."

"You should make notes, like Margaret does and then you wouldn't forget," Karen said.

"Funny coming from a woman who loses her keys every few minutes and has been blind, deaf and dumb at least three times." And the Dames were off and running.

Margaret, always sensitive to the needs of her friends, decided to let them chat while she served the refreshments.

"Now Dames, it's back to business."

"That pie was delicious," Karen said. "So, Margaret, we've heard from everyone except you."

"I did give you a condo decor report, but I was saving the best part. When I called Mr. Miller to set up the appointment, he asked out of the blue if I baked. Then he said he'd meet with me if I brought lemon bars. Apparently Edith was a baker as well as a cash cow. While he was getting the tea ready, I snooped around. His bookcase was lined with pictures of young women. I wouldn't call them beautiful exactly, but they did have a distinct look: All of them had a lot of long hair and were heavily made up. You know what I mean, like those ads for glamour photos. He mentioned Tiffany as one of his success stories."

"Could those be family members—kids, grandkids, nieces?" Lynn asked.

"The Millers never had children of their own," Susan said. "Edith and her first husband had two sons. I don't know about grandkids or nieces."

"I didn't see any pictures of young men, but I didn't get back to the master bedroom. I did, however, get to the guest bath as per my instructions. And I did find something interesting in the medicine cabinet: a prescription for birth control pills. Mr. Miller might still be pimping right out of his condo!"

"That disgusting old man! I knew he was more than a cat killer," Lynn said. "See, girls, I was right to nominate him."

"I'm not quite finished," Margaret interrupted. "As I was leaving, he asked me for a hug. Can you believe it?"

"I can. You've still got it, Margaret. Did you hug him? Give me the dirt, girlfriend," Lynn said.

"Are you kidding me? He made my skin crawl. I got out of there as fast as I could and went right home and took a shower. I still get freaked out, just thinking about it. Okay, Dames, let's brainstorm. Susan, would you please take notes so we can all have copies? I'll write the info down on the whiteboard so we can all see it."

"Let's do it!"

The Dames bounced facts, observations, and inferences off each other like Powerball numbers in a barrel.

> 1. 'Mentored' young women (Tiffany) displayed their pictures got T's name from a frat brother, guy from restaurant?
>
> 2. Hard of hearing
>
> 3. Ran over a cat
>
> 4. Liked lemon bars, tea, spaghetti, and Johnny Cash

"Don't forget he loves martinis. He had two when we had lunch the first time," Lynn volunteered.

"Good. Feel free to interrupt with new info at any time," Margaret said, adding martinis to number four.

> 5. Allergic to nuts and chocolate
>
> 6. Dead wife (Edith had money)
>
> 7. Cheap, rude, creepy, etc.
>
> 8. Bad taste (condo, clothing, hair plugs)
>
> 9. Bad friends (frat boys from the U)
>
> 10. No kids
>
> 11. Has money
>
> 12. Aspirin and birth control pills in medicine cabinet, young woman still living there?
>
> 13. Has maid/cleaning woman (young woman living there?)
>
> 14. Said women got ugly as they age

"What nerve, coming from a man with fake teeth and hair plugs," Karen said.

15. Liked young women

16. Aka Bobby Big Boy Miller, served some time for pimping

17. Made his money in sales

18. Took money from George, friends with others at table?

19. Helped fund Marco's restaurant

20. Owns a Porsche

"Anything else, Dames? We can always add to the list. Now for the fun part. Given the info we've gathered, do you have ideas for the extermination?"

"How about we ask him for dinner and serve Thai food?" Susan, the cook and stir fry expert, suggested.

"I don't get it," Karen said. She was a meat and potatoes kind of girl.

"Thai food often uses peanut oil and peanuts," Margaret explained.

"Ah," Karen said. "Peanut allergies. My sweet granddaughter's school has signs up all over the building: 'This is a peanut free school.' Do you girls remember anything about peanut allergies when you were a kid?" The Dames shook their heads. "I think the species is weakening."

"Not the 'species is weakening' thing again. We've heard that a million times, haven't we girls?" Susan looked at her partners in crime.

"How about arranging a cat bite and then putting something in the wound that would cause septicemia. I like the idea of a cat doing him in. After all, that's what he did to that poor cat," Lynn said. "I could volunteer Butch; he has all his teeth and his claws. Plus he's perpetually pissed off."

"I saw a cool murder on TV using the wire from a pair of circular knitting needles. I have those in a wide variety of sizes. You just come up from behind, and slip the wire around his head ... "

"We get it, Karen. No need to get all graphic on us. Remember we're delicate exterminators."

"Okay, how's this for 'delicate'? How about something like a poisonous tea made from some toxic plants. I could do some research on toxic plants. Since I have a greenhouse in my condo, I could certainly expand my collection of exotics," Lynn volunteered.

"Way to go, Toxic!"

"Does anyone know anything about cars? Could we cut off his power steering or brakes? He does love that car."

"I like the idea of exploiting his sexual adventures. The only trouble is we're too old and too 'ugly' for his tastes."

"I can guarantee he wouldn't get excited about a paraplegic, thank God," Susan said.

Lynn paused and looked directly at Margaret. "But he might get excited about you, Margaret. After all, he wanted a hug."

"Oh, no you don't. I'm not going near that despicable, perverted man."

"Wait, ladies. Margaret doesn't have to do anything sexual. She just needs to have access to him and his condo," Susan said.

"Susan, is there any way you can hack into his medical records like you did with the attorney? Maybe there would be something we could use." Margaret was grasping at straws, hoping to avoid anything up close and personal with Bobby Big Boy Miller. Just thinking about it made her skin crawl.

"I think we've done enough this session. We'll meet again next week. Now we need to do some serious thinking about how we're going to exterminate this asshole or in Lynn-speak his 'assholiness.'"

The Dames gasped because Margaret was not one to curse.

CHAPTER 8

Choose Your Poison

The week flew by with the Dames reveling in their research about ways to "eliminate" their neighbor, aka his Assholiness. They found it quite invigorating and all agreed it made them feel young and alive, a vivid contrast to their client's future.

They would get together informally over lunch, most often at Susan's since she actually cooked, to chat about various garroting or defenestration techniques, all in purely abstract, hypothetical terms, you understand. They wanted to explore various nonviolent extermination possibilities without getting into specifics. Nonviolent meant clean, no noise and no struggles. They would also prefer not having to watch. Dying should be done in private, after all.

This afternoon's lunch of homemade pizza and a tossed salad was destined to get more specific. Susan had opened a bottle of her favorite red blend just in case the Dames wanted to break their no drinking while planning rule. They did.

"I still say thirty-six inch circular needles, you know the kind I use for my afghans, would be quite efficient," Karen volunteered. "Or one of those flexible dog leashes..."

"And what's delicate about that, girlfriend?" Lynn interrupted. "Garroting is messy business and you'd have to be strong and quiet to come up behind the victim. Since I've lost so much weight ... "

At that the Dames hooted in unison because Lynn was an infamous yo-yo dieter. Down ten up fifteen. She was currently on an upswing.

"Defenestration is much less messy, especially if the person is tossed from a considerable height. We would only see the mess from a distance," Margaret, commented.

"We could invite him to dinner, serve him a couple of dirty martinis and invite him out to the deck. Margaret, you could weaken some of the guardrails and make sure he's close to the weakened ones. Maybe he could be leaning against the rail and you could lean in to kiss him. Then you could give him a little push. He was drunk, after all. Then we wouldn't see it at all. It would just be an unfortunate accident."

"Lean in to kiss him? Lynn, are you crazy? With my luck I'd try to kiss the sleaze, he'd move out of the way and I'd be the one splattered on the pavement. No way." The thought of their dear friend "splattered on the pavement" was sobering. Not comfortable with the long silence, Lynn continued.

"Did I tell you about my latest visit to my ophthalmologist?" Lynn asked. Lynn was famous for her *non sequiturs*, the word *see* most likely causing that one. The Dames attributed it to old age onset ADD."

"You have cataracts in both eyes," the Dames answered in unison. It seemed Lynn was fixated on her eyesight, understandable at her age.

"Okay, okay, maybe I obsess a bit about my eyes." Lynn paused to clean her glasses.

"At least it's a pleasant change from revisiting your hip replacement surgery. Actually I prefer cataracts," Karen said.

"Good thing, because you've probably got them too. My doctor says everyone gets them."

"Okay, point made."

"What about poisons? Since you don't seem to like my balcony scenario. I was researching plants that would cause heart problems. Did you know rhubarb leaves can kill? Or that the Dieffenbachia plant in the lobby is poisonous?"

"*Death by Dieffenbachia*, great title for a mystery," Susan said as she passed a big bowl of salad greens.

"Also, one castor bean can cause death. And then there's oleander and nightshade—lots of possibilities with poison."

"I saw an episode of *Damages* where one of the bad guys was killed by an overdose of potassium," Margaret volunteered.

"This pizza is delicious, Susan. I love the Feta cheese," Lynn commented, once again switching topics.

"Aren't bananas filled with potassium? I could make him banana bread with twice the bananas..."

"Banana overdose: very funny, Susan," Margaret commented.

"How about poison mushrooms? I loved the wild mushroom ravioli at Costello's. Maybe we could find some poisonous 'shrooms and bring Mr. Miller a delicious dinner. Takeout Poison."

"Another great title for a book. Not a bad thought about the mushrooms, Lynn, but where would we get poisonous mushrooms?" Margaret asked.

"I'll check the Internet and see what I can find. You can find out how to build a bomb; you should be able to find out how to find poison 'shrooms," Susan said, wheeling to the living room where she kept her computer. "You guys keep eating your lunch."

The Dames did just that, carefully picking out the mushrooms on the homemade pizza, hiding them discreetly in their napkins. If they were good at anything besides knocking off deserving old coots, they were good at eating.

"Here's the skinny, girls. There are lots of poisonous mushrooms out there, but there is one that grows locally, something called the false morel that looks very much like the real thing except it causes nausea, diarrhea, severe headaches. It could even put him in a coma."

"But can it kill him? That is, after all, the reason for all this," Karen interrupted.

"It might take seven to ten days, but yes, it can kill him, especially since he's elderly. I would suspect the dying would be horrific. We might want to reconsider. We do pride ourselves on restraint. Delicacy is our motto after all."

"Oh, I don't know. A little old fashioned suffering might be good for Mr. Miller's soul, if he has one," Karen added.

"I kind of like imagining Mr. Miller with the Mexican quick step," Lynn said, grinning.

"And defiling the Laura Ashley bathrooms. Poop and peonies, such a delightful combo," Karen said, adding to the sophomoric humor.

"Girls, girls, we're trying to eat here," Margaret said. "So tell us how to tell the difference between the 'good guys' and the 'bad guys.'"

"I've always loved the 'bad guys' myself," Karen of the three husbands said. "I remember George and how he loved to---"

"Garden," Susan interrupted before Karen could elaborate. "Here's how you tell the poisonous morel from the delicious one, according to the May 7, *Star Tribune:*"

> *There is, however, a false morel, called*
> *Gyromitra. The biggest difference is the solid or*
> *fibrous stem and round, uneven rounded cap*
> *with folds. It's edible in some, but not all*
> *regions, and can be toxic. At first glance it may*
> *resemble a morel, but upon closer inspection, the*
> *differences in stem and cap become clear. If*
> *there's any doubt, do not pick or eat these.*

"Unless, of course, you want to knock off an asshole," Lynn said.

"Where do you find these 'false' morels?" Margaret asked.

"They like the same environment as the real morels," Susan continued. "Again from the *Strib:*"

Seek morels in uncompacted soil, the ashes of a
forest fire, near stands of aspen and birch, young
second growths of hardwood, near recently dead
or dying elms or spruce stumps. They also like
the edges of conifer forests, walnut and
butternut trees, as well as old apple orchards.
You might spot them on the banks of rivers and
streams, along drainages of ravines, game trails.

"So there might be some close by," Margaret said.

"Right you are, Margaret. Since we live on a river and are close to a state park, it sounds to me like you girls are going to experience a destination event!" Susan laughed. The rest of the Dames groaned.

"Even as a kid I hated field trips," Lynn said as she downed her second glass of a domestic red blend.

"I can use a refill as well. Pass the bottle, Lynn," Karen said. "May I freshen your drink, Margaret?"

"You'd better believe it. A toast to our 'destination' event!"

"There are times I just love being disabled," Susan said as she clinked glasses with her pals.

* * *

A-hunting we will go, a-hunting we will go

(Heigh-ho, the derry-o, a-hunting we will go

A-hunting we will go, a-hunting we will go)

We'll catch a creep and put him to sleep

And then we won't let him go.

"All this pathetic singing reminds me of road trips when I was a kid," Karen said. "Only without my brothers poking me. I hated road trips then and I hate them now."

"This hardly qualifies as a road trip. We've only been driving fifteen minutes," Margaret said.

The girls continued singing unenthusiastically until

Margaret pulled her candy apple red Mustang hard top into the Fort Snelling State Park Visitor Center's parking lot.

"Does this mean we have to get out of the car?" Lynn said.

"Quit whining. Remember we're doing this to exterminate Mr. Miller. Keep your eyes on the prize, girlfriend," Karen said. She was wearing a big straw hat, her usual too small hand knit cardigan and a pair of khaki capris. Slip on white tennis shoes completed the look.

"Yeah, whatever." Lynn struggled to extricate herself from the sports car's small back seat. "Margaret, why don't you get yourself a four door so that your friends can be more comfortable?" Lynn made one of those elderly poofy sounds as she finally got out of the car.

For her "field trip" ensemble, Lynn was wearing a short-sleeved, v-necked knit top and capri pants from a fashionable boutique. She carried a big canvas LL Bean bag. Her jewelry was rather simple: a gold chain and hoop earrings to match. Her shoes: sparkly flip flops.

"Getting a little stiff and noisy in your old age," Karen commented from outside the car.

"Easy for you to say. You got to sit in the front seat. I get dibs on the front seat for the ride home."

"Now that reminds me of road trips when I was a kid — always fighting for the best seats. Well, girls, we're here. Let's check things out in the Center, pay our fees, use the restrooms. Lynn, do we have everything? Library books, bottled water, insect repellant, sunscreen, granola bars, bags for the mushrooms?"

"All present and accounted for," Lynn announced.

" Let's do it!" Karen said.

"Good, but promise me no more singing," Margaret said.

After a half hour of reading about Minnesota history and Park Rules and Regs, they exited the building ready for some serious 'shroom sleuthing.

"What's this about not taking anything from the park grounds? What about getting the shrooms home? What if we get picked up by the mushroom cops? I can't have a police record at my age." Lynn, who planned murders, was totally unaware of the irony.

Let's face it: The Dames weren't exactly the camping, tromping through the woods type of women. The great outdoors was as foreign to them as poverty. The most rustic accommodations any of them had ever endured was a weekend or two at a Country Inn Suite. And they were old and definitely outside their comfort zones, especially Margaret, dressed in a linen sundress and strapped sandals, looking like she was going to lunch at the St. Paul Hotel. Mosquitos formed a halo around her head.

About a mile or so into the hike after finding no fungi whatever, Lynn decided to read to the Dames. "How about a little mushroom trivia? It might make this walk a little less boring. Ready?"

"Ready," the girls said in unison.

"What do you call a mushroom specialist?"

"A fun-gi," Margaret said, laughing. Karen snorted.

"No, a mycologist, but your joke was pretty funny. That could be the punch line for a lot jokes like 'What do you call a mycologist with a ten-inch penis?"

"A fun-gi," they said in unison.

Just then something slithered across the path. Margaret, who was traumatized by a garter snake as a child, screamed, jumped, and twisted her ankle, falling onto the path.

Lynn subsequently tripped while trying to avoid Margaret and fell into a patch of what looked very much like poison ivy.

"Are you okay, Margaret?"

"I think I really hurt my ankle. I don't think I can walk."

"Hey, I'm flat on my keister too. But don't bother with me. I'm fine, thank you very much."

"All you've done is whine. Make yourself useful and call for help, Lynn."

"Help!" Lynn yelled.

"I meant use your phone to call for help."

"Oh, shit, was that on our list? Maybe I put it in and forgot." Lynn grabbed her canvas bag, threw the food, water, plastic bags, hand wipes, books, sunscreen, bug spray, and a picture of Butch, her favorite cat, onto the ground and rummaged through the contents. No phone. "Anyone for a bottle of water and a granola bar?" Lynn got to her hands and knees and looked expectantly at Karen.

"No way I'm helping you," Karen said. "You landed in poison ivy and might be contagious, but I will repack your bag."

"What a pal," Lynn said as she grunted her way to her feet.

CHAPTER 9

Is the ER a 'destination' event?

After about fifteen minutes of Margaret's hobbling while holding onto Karen with Lynn close behind yelling "Help," the Dames were rescued by a couple of middle-aged male hikers who happened to have a cell phone. A quick call to the Center and they were picked up in a golf cart and taken to Margaret's car. With a lot of help, they got Margaret comfortable in the back seat where she elevated her foot.

"Now what?" Margaret said through clenched teeth. "This ankle hurts like the devil." She was pale and looked like she might faint.

"I'll drive you to the ER at United Hospital," Karen said as she got into the car. "Any other requests?"

"I'll take that bottle of water now and the granola bar." Lynn handed the food and water to Margaret. "On second thought, just the water. I feel nauseous."

"I feel so guilty about not bringing my cell phone," Lynn said.

"It wasn't just you. None of us remembered. You'll be okay once we get to the hospital. It's probably just a bad sprain," Karen said as she pulled out onto Highway 5.

"Are we there yet?" Margaret asked in an attempt to lighten the mood.

Twenty minutes later they were checking into the ER. After filling out the necessary paperwork, Margaret was seen by a doctor and sent for x-rays where it was discovered she had fractured her ankle. She was then moved by wheelchair to orthopedics on the fourth floor. And then she met Dr. Thomas Bedlow.

A small, wiry older man with his own hair and teeth, both must haves on the Dames' wish list, bustled into the room with a white lab coat open to a light yellow shirt, pressed dress pants, a stethoscope dangling around his neck. He took one look at Margaret and grinned, displaying beautiful teeth and dimples.

Karen looked at Lynn and mouthed, *Dimples. I just love dimples.*

"Doctor Thomas Bedlow at your service." The good doctor shook hands all around. "I assume you're the patient." He looked at Margaret with interest. "Would you like me to call you Mrs. Thompson or Margaret?"

"Margaret will be fine. I'm a widow and I think of Mrs. Thompson as my late mother-in-law."

"Then Margaret it will be," he said, smiling. "Tell me what happened here."

"Well, my friends and I were walking in Fort Snelling Park and a snake slithered across our paths. I hate snakes and I jumped. In the process I twisted my ankle."

"And I fell on my keister," Lynn volunteered, looking dewy eyed at Dr. Tom while scratching her hands and arms. They were red, blistered, and weeping a clear fluid.

"Can I see your hands?"

"You can call me Lynn," Lynn said, holding out her hands and arms. Doctor Tom was careful not to get too close. She looked down at the blisters with a shocked expression. "Oh, crap, this has gotten much worse." Karen and Margaret smiled, knowing that Lynn had cleaned up her language for the doctor.

"You have poison ivy and need to get some medication. I'll write down some over-the-counter treatments. You can also make a paste of oatmeal to help ease the itching." He handed Lynn the list. Lynn looked disappointed that he didn't show her more concern. *Maybe he was on the autism/ Asperger's scale like that British Doc Martin.* She tried again.

"Are you sure it's not something more serious? Shingles maybe? Hailey-Hailey disease? I was a nurse, you know. Should I make an appointment with you?" Lynn batted her eyelashes and looked hopeful. She'd always had a thing for doctors.

"For God's sake, Lynn, shingles on your hands? Hailey-Hailey? He's a orthopedic doctor not a dermatologist. Don't play the stupid old lady card with Dr. Tom," Karen admonished. Not once did Dr. Tom look away from Margaret. He was as focused on Margaret as Lynn was on him. Margaret was in too much pain to react to either of her friends.

"Now for you, Margaret. The x-rays show a fracture in your ankle, but I'd also like x-rays of your foot in case you might have broken something there as well. I'll meet you back here when you're finished. I'll call the nurse to take you to x-ray. Ladies." He made a quick exit, leaving the faint smell of hand soap behind. A nurse entered the exam room as the doctor exited.

"I just love the smell of hand soap. It reminds me of the days when I was a nurse saving lives in the ER. I remember this one doctor..." Lynn trailed off into Lynn Land where reality was nonexistent. Karen just rolled her eyes.

"Mrs. Thompson, my name is Jacky and I'll be taking you for x-rays if you promise no jokes about *Nurse Jackie*."

Margaret laughed. "No worries. I never really got into that show. Too many drugs, all those pain killers that are so addictive. Nothing more than Ibuprofen for me."

"You might change your mind in a few hours."

"Good luck," Karen said as her dear friend was wheeled away.

"Wasn't he just the cutest thing? Did you see his dimples? And I noticed no wedding ring. Wouldn't it be great if Margaret could hook up with a doctor?"

"You weren't thinking of Margaret a few minutes ago. You went absolutely gaga over the guy in the white coat. Some things never change," Karen said.

"At least I haven't been married three times," Lynn said, scratching like crazy.

Karen ignored the marriage slam; she was used to it.

"Isn't poison ivy contagious?" Karen asked. "Do I need to worry about your infecting all of us with that disgusting rash?"

"Not really. The blister juice isn't contagious, but I might still have some of the oil from the plant on my clothes."

"'Blister juice'! Very technical terms for a nurse. And a gardener at that!"

"I'm more into tropical plants, not common plants like poison ivy. Plus, I didn't have time for plant analysis before I fell. That damn slippery, slimy reptile scared me half to death." The Dames settled in with out-of-date *People* magazines to keep them company until Margaret returned.

"Just how many articles do we need to read about Jennifer Aniston and Angelina Jolie anyway?" Karen said.

Just then Nurse Jacky wheeled Margaret back into the room.

"After the doctor looks at the x-rays, I'll be showing you how to use crutches and how to use the boot. The doctor will talk to you about treatment and further visits." Nurse Jacky took one look at Lynn and said, "Nasty rash. Looks like poison ivy to me."

"Ah shit," Lynn said scratching. Nurse Jacky chuckled as she left the room.

"How are you feeling, Margaret?" Karen said.

"My foot and ankle throb along with my head. Slightly woozy with the possibility of fainting," Margaret said, looking very pale.

Doctor Tom entered just as Margaret was about to pass out. He pushed her head down, but still managed to hold on so she wouldn't fall out of the wheelchair. After a minute or two, her color started to return to normal.

"Ladies, I would like to talk to Margaret privately for a few minutes if you don't mind. You can wait outside in the family area just down the hall to your left."

"I wonder what that's about?" Lynn asked. "Don't you think it's kind of weird?" Just then the proverbial light bulb went on and Lynn gasped. "He's going to ask her out! I just knew it. I saw the way he was looking at her."

"Have you noticed how Margaret can still look beautiful no matter what? Look at today. Her dress still looks good. I mean how can linen not wrinkle? And there's not a hair out of place. The wig helps, of course, but wouldn't you think the wig would have moved a bit when she fell? Speaking of wigs, why does she always wear them? Have you seen her with her real hair?"

"I asked her once about the wigs and she said it was because she was beginning to get bald. And no, I've never seen her without her wig. With or without a wig, she's amazing.

I remember the time she got the flu and I brought her some soup. She was sitting up in bed, looking like she had just returned from the beauty parlor. Unbelievable! And she had a fever of over 101 and was coughing like she had whooping cough. Just once I would like to see her disheveled and unattractive." Lynn paused and then continued. "It must be hard to be Margaret, to think that your value is in the way you look. She's got to be under a lot of pressure. Now that women are able to postpone aging with beauty products and cosmetic surgery, we can be younger looking much longer. But when can we relax and not worry about being judged for our looks? When is it safe to be old? When is it safe to be married for that matter?"

When Karen looked up from her magazine, Lynn was lost in a memory...

"Michelle, this is Lynn, Ben's wife."

"I know who you are. What do you want?"

*"I know you and Ben are having an affair.
Please stop seeing him. If you have any
decency at all---"*

*"Ben is here. Why don't you talk to him?
Darling, your hysterical wife is on the phone."*

*I can hear you. I can hear you. Why can't you
hear me?*

"You're remembering Ben, aren't you? I can always tell. You seem so sad and far away."

"You know me well. He wanted someone younger and more attractive," Lynn said. "I was never enough."

"He was a narcissistic ass, not worthy of you," Karen said.

"Thanks for saying that. Still, there should a safe time for us where we can be ourselves, not all made up or dressed to the nines. Just look at us. We should have been dressed in our old jeans or shorts, wearing sensible shoes, not flip flops and strappy sandals. Instead we cover our flabby arms and thighs and our varicose veins. We undermine ourselves when we buy into that shit. After twenty-five years, I should have been safe. Fuck it! I'm going to stop dieting and reading *People* magazine!"

"Thatta girl! Now you sound like yourself! For the cause, I'm taking off this stupid cardigan and flapping these old flabby arms right in front of Dr. Dimples!"

About ten minutes later Margaret was wheeled in, pale and shaky, but still beautiful. "Well, women, are you ready to watch me negotiate crutches and the boot? The boot actually feels good. You can add air to make it fit your ankle perfectly." Margaret demonstrated boot technology to her friends.

"Now for the crutches," Margaret said as she awkwardly negotiated a few steps. "Good thing I have a one level unit and elevators. Otherwise, I'd have to bump up and down the steps on my bottom."

"What did the doctor say?" Lynn asked, winking at Karen.

"Well, I have to come back every week or so for x-rays to see if the bones are healing."

"Bones as in plural?" Lynn asked, her nurse's training finally kicking in.

"Apparently there are several broken bones in the foot and one in my ankle. I might need surgery if they don't heal on their own. I have to stay off the foot for about two weeks which means I wear the boot and use the crutches. When I get the go ahead, I can just use the ugly ol' boot."

"How about a walker?" Karen suggested. "It might be easier than the crutches. Or a wheelchair."

"Those are for old people!"

"Hate to break it to you, sweetie, but we are old people," Karen said.

"Shush, I'm already in pain. I don't need you to add to it. I'm ready to go home," Margaret said. "I might as well use the wheelchair since it's here. I don't think I could make it on crutches."

The orderly pushed Margaret all the way to the emergency room entrance where Karen was waiting with Margaret's red Mustang. Once Lynn was situated in the back seat, the orderly positioned Margaret, commented on the "cool" car, and wheeled the chair back for some other unfortunate.

"'Destination event' my ass," Lynn said under her breath, her ample ass stuffed uncomfortably in the back seat.

"Then let's get the hell outta Dodge," Karen said. "I'll get you two settled at home and go to the drugstore to get something for the poison ivy and fill Margaret's prescription. You girls can chill in the meantime. Order in some lunch, have a glass of wine. Once you start taking the strong stuff, you won't be able to drink. Be sure to fill Susan in on our outing."

"I don't intend to take any of the strong stuff. I'm just letting you be helpful."

"You say that now, but when your throbbing foot and

ankle keep you awake, you'll be happy to have the Vicodin, at least for the next couple of days. Then you can throw the pills away or sell them and make yourself some cash."

"Margaret as a drug pusher—just can't see it," Karen said, laughing.

"Besides the pills make you constipated," Lynn added.

"Great, won't be able to poop, won't be able to walk," Margaret said under her breath. "Thanks. I appreciate all your help. You're the best friends ever," Margaret said, closing her eyes.

"We'll be home in a jiffy," Karen said.

CHAPTER 10

Let the Pity Party Begin!

"Susan, when you get this message call Margaret's apartment. Margaret's had a little accident, nothing terribly serious, but it will slow things down a bit."

Susan heard the message as she wheeled out of the bathroom after taking a long, hot shower. All she had to do was get dressed, which was easy for her because she didn't care how she looked.

She did, however, look pretty "hot" when she and her apartment were featured in *Minnesota Monthly,* proving that the handicapped could be as attractive and live in as much luxury and comfort as the rest of the privileged one percent.

In addition to practical considerations like pull up bars, strategically placed poles, lowered counters, and wider doorways, Susan insisted on having beauty surround her. With help from a well-known interior design team, she displayed original acrylic and watercolor paintings, lithographs, and silk screens, along with functional and decorative pottery, all by well-known local artists. Add expensive fabrics and window treatments, a mixture of antiques with comfortable upholstered pieces and you had a unique home Susan seldom cared to leave. With her financial means she could afford the best and the most beautiful. Why not? She deserved it after all that she had endured.

Of course, it helped that Susan was wealthy and somewhat famous because the man who caused her permanent disability was a very high profile elected official. And a drunk. Not wanting any more negative publicity, said official agreed to a very generous settlement, provided Susan didn't make a huge public fuss. She complied up to a point. She made enough of a public fuss to make sure the jerk wasn't reelected. Add that settlement to her prior financial success and Susan was one wealthy Dame. Unfortunately, wealth didn't insure her happiness.

Before Susan left her apartment to visit Margaret, she ordered an expensive bouquet of Margaret's favorite lilies to be delivered later. And a bouquet for herself as well. Flowers always cheered her up, not so much as her monthly bank statements and stock reports, but they would do nicely for a minor crisis like Margaret's "accident."

Susan didn't bother to knock or ring the bell. "I got your message. What's happened?" One look at Margaret and she knew it wasn't good. "Margaret, how are you?"

"You wouldn't believe all the shit that has happened," Lynn said as she was pacing the floor scratching her arms. She went on to describe in boring detail the mushroom debacle, the snake, the falls, the "cute boys" who rescued them, the hospital, the poison ivy, Nurse Jacky, Doctor Tom who fell for Margaret, blah, blah, blah.

"You left out your drooling over Dr. Tom and trying to get him to treat your 'shingles,'" Karen added, holding the drugstore bag in her hand. "These should help." Margaret was sitting in her Eames leather chair with her booted foot resting on the ottoman. She looked pale and rather frail, but as always, she smiled and asked if Susan would like a beverage.

"I'll have what she's having," Susan said, quoting a line from *When Harry Met Sally,* one of their favorite movies. Karen brought Susan an iced tea.

"Karen, would you please bring me some crackers and cheese and a refill on my wine?"

"Get it yourself. You can walk."

"But my arms and hands itch," Lynn said in that whiny tone she was famous for.

"Put on some more lotion and quit complaining," Karen said. "Everything is not always about you."

"Or you."

"Give it a rest, you two. Margaret doesn't need this."

"But she does need this," Karen said, handing her a pain pill. "This should help. Remember the doctor said you should keep on top of the pain. Every four hours for a few days. No need to tough it out."

"So says Nurse Karen. Even though I am a real nurse, not a nurse wannabe like some people. I can see that Fake Nurse Karen has it all under control." She gave Karen The Look. "It's time I went home to my cats who happen to love me unconditionally, unlike certain other people I can mention." Staring at Karen, Lynn puffed out her ample chest, held her head high and made her exit, letting a little toot as she did so.

"Wow, that was dramatic! I especially liked the exit fart," Susan said, laughing. "So, Margaret, how are you really feeling?"

"Exhausted, achy, and disappointed the mission was not accomplished. I just wish I could go to sleep and wake up. Nightmare over." She looked at Susan in her wheelchair.

"Sorry. That was totally insensitive of me."

"No apology needed. I get it."

"Thanks, you've all been so good to me. Even Lynn. Do you think she'll get over her little snit?"

"She always does. Just give her a little time," Karen said, "and enjoy the sweet silence."

"I think I'll lie down for awhile and let the drugs do their magic." Karen got up to help, but Margaret waved her away. "I've got to get used to these damn things." Karen followed to make sure she got to bed safely.

"Karen, you must be tired as well. Why don't you go home

for a couple of hours to get some rest yourself? I'll stay until she wakes up.

By the way, I ordered some flowers for Margaret. They should be arriving in the next few hours."

"Great idea! If you don't mind, I'll take you up on the offer. I could use a nap."

A few hours later Karen returned with an overnight bag. "I'll stay with her tonight until she feels more confident using the crutches."

"You're a good friend, Karen."

"'Right back at ya' as my grandkids say."

While Susan was alone, her mind traveled to her accident and all the pain and sadness that caused, the friends and family whose lives were also affected. Margaret's accident had triggered painful memories. She needed to get home.

The first thing Susan did once she was back in her own apartment was go to her desk and pull out the folder containing all the newspaper articles and the letters from Steve, her former lover and fiancé, who bailed after realizing he didn't want to be shackled to a cripple for the rest of his life.

After reading all the letters again, including the one terminating their relationship, Susan realized she still had feelings for Steve. She alternated between "I'm better off without the bastard" to intense longing for the life they had planned before the accident changed everything. At the time, she was heartbroken. She felt alone and scared. After several surgeries, months of rehab, and counseling, Susan finally accepted her situation and tried to make the best of it, without Steve or the hope of a future relationship with any man.

Susan wheeled herself into the kitchen and poured herself a glass of her favorite red blend. *I deserve it after reading all those damn letters and seeing Margaret hurt and in pain. After all it's Happy Hour somewhere.* She drank the first glass, poured herself a second, turned on her favorite Bill Evans CD and wheeled into the living room. She took the bottle with her and wheeled to her computer to do what she did best.

>Steve Gilbert, aged sixty-six, Chicago
>architect, founded Gilbert and Sullivan
>Contemporary Design ... winner of the Green
>Design Award ... noted speaker for
>environmentally friendly home designs ...
>scheduled to speak at the Minneapolis Home
>and Garden show in February.

Gilbert and Sullivan, you've got to be kiddin' me. Who'd name an architectural firm after those Victorian lightweights? Guess I know the answer to that question. Maybe a little green cottage for Yum-Yum. Susan hooted at the thought.

She went deeper into her research. No felonies, no arrests, no DUIs, just a few parking tickets. *Way to keep your nose clean, Steve. Now for the big question: Are you married? Did you delete me and move on?*

Bingo. "Steve Gilbert married socialite, Mary Carter, in 2011 and divorced in 2013." *A socialite? I can't imagine you'd be happy with a rich, entitled, spoiled brat! Wonder if she liked camping, roughing it in nature, swatting mosquitoes, using a porta potty, showering in communal showers. I remember lots of good times in your pop up camper—the bird watching, the star gazing, making love, bumping our heads on the roof, and laughing. Most of all we laughed. We were best friends.*

It was all so romantic. Susan was beginning to get maudlin, one step from the ugly weepies, all part of the Pity Party.

Maybe I should go to the Home and Garden show, maybe meet him for a drink or two. Maybe I should send him an e-mail. God, woman, what are you thinking? Susan poured more wine. *Yup, that's what I'll do. I'll put the ball in his court. It's up to him.* After numerous attempts, Susan settled on this impersonal, emotionally empty e-mail.

>*Steve,*
>
>*Congrats on the award.*

Best,

Susan

Susan finished her third glass, closed her eyes, said a little prayer, and pressed send.

Good Lord, what have I done? I should know better than to drink and e-mail. She paused and then poured the last of the bottle. *Whatever. What's done is done. Okay, I'm sick of the Pity Party, though it was fun while it lasted. Now it's on to bigger and better things. Nap first; plan murder second.*

Susan wheeled into her bedroom, took two aspirin, and drank a large glass of water.

CHAPTER 11

Aspirin anyone? Or Plan B

"Ladies, hush. We've got business to conduct," Margaret said, tapping her iced tea glass to get the Dames' attention. The Dames totally ignored her as usual, laughing and chatting amiably. Instead of standing, Margaret was seated with her leg elevated. Maybe that's why they ignored her.

Margaret didn't understand. Her friends were so attentive to her every need since the accident; grocery shopping, doctor's appointments, food preparation, helping with the household chores, but they couldn't keep their traps shut. *This must be what a teacher experiences every day.* Margaret remembered her seventh grade English teacher, Miss Martini, who patiently stood quietly in front of the class, trying to get their attention. It seemed an eternity to Margaret who was a stellar student and Miss Martini's favorite. When Miss Martini had had enough, she would yell, "Shut up!" Amazingly they did.

So Margaret channeled Miss Martini, struggled to her feet and stood quietly for several minutes before she yelled, "Shut up!" The yell was so forceful she almost lost her balance. The Dames saw her falter and immediately stopped their senseless chatter and gave Margaret their full attention. *Finally.*

"Since the Mushroom Project was a total failure, I think we need to consider a Plan B."

"It wasn't a total failure. You got to meet Dr. Tom," Lynn said.

"There is that," Margaret said, blushing. *If they only knew.* "Any suggestions?"

"I've been thinking quite a bit about our client, Mr. Miller, and I think I have a pretty good idea," Susan said.

"Spill it, girlfriend," Lynn said as she helped herself to another slice of strawberry cheese cake. "To hell with the diet."

"You know how Mr. Miller used to 'mentor' young women? Well, why don't we hire one of those young women to help Margaret in her time of need."

"'Time of need?' Aren't you being a little overly dramatic? I'm momentarily vulnerable, that's all. In a few weeks I'll be just fine, though I must admit not being able to drive is problematic."

"And what if you need surgery? Remember the doctor said if you did have surgery, you would be off your feet for six weeks."

"We can deal with that when and if it happens, Susan."

"In the meantime you could use the help, especially with the driving. And we could use a little help with Mr. Miller if we're going to pull this extermination off.

Tiffany or Buffy or whatever silly name she might have, could be our mole, our inside look at Miller's health, his meds, his daily life. She could be a real source of valuable information, in addition to helping you. It sounds like a twofer to me."

"Wait a minute, Susan, shouldn't I have a say in this? I'm not sure I want a stranger looking after me in my 'time of need.' I seem to be managing quite well, with your help, of course."

"Hear me out, Margaret. You are so good at getting people to confide in you that I'm sure you'd get some good information." Susan knew Margaret's weakness: She loved flattery.

"You're right. I am good at drawing people out. For the sake of argument, let's say we get this 'good' info about his meds. For example, maybe we find out he is taking a statin for high cholesterol. Maybe we decide we're going to tamper with his meds. We'd need access to the apartment. Right?"

"I've got an idea," Karen said. "We could get into Tiffany or Buffy's purse, take her keys, and make duplicates." The Dames rolled their eyes at Karen's outrageous plan.

"If Tiffany or Buffy still had the keys to Bob's apartment. If T or B is still living with him... " Susan responded.

"Remember I did find the birth control pills in Bob's guest bathroom," Margaret said. "That seems to be evidence that one of his 'girls' is still living there."

"Unless Mr. Miller was using them himself. I read about estrogen therapy for prostate cancer. It blocks testosterone, but doesn't cure the cancer. It just slows the progression. But I don't know if the estrogen would be administered in that form," Lynn said, embracing her inner nurse.

"It will be your job, Lynn, to research that very question," Susan said.

Lynn nodded.

"Estrogen therapy—my God, I'm surprised the man didn't grow man boobs living in that apartment; the decorating couldn't have been more blatantly feminine. I start to hyperventilate just thinking about it," said Margaret.

"Wouldn't it be ironic if Mr. Miller had advanced prostate cancer? We wouldn't have to do much of anything except wait and watch," Lynn said.

"Don't count on it. I'm betting the old geezer is fairly healthy," Karen said.

"Back to my suggestion. If we do use one of his 'girls,' one of us will have to approach him to make the contact. Margaret, you'd be the likely choice because you're the one needing the help and you've talked to him several times before, and since you're temporarily indisposed, he should come to you. Ask if one of the 'girls' was still living with him. You know, emphasize how convenient it would be for both of you," Susan said.

"Oh, no you don't. I don't want to be near that dirty old man, especially now. He tried to hug me last time. It took days and many showers before I could shake that memory," said Margaret.

"One of us could be here, if that would help," Karen said.

"Promise? I don't want to be alone with him." The Dames nodded in agreement.

"Remember you do have crutches to use as weapons," Lynn said, laughing at the image of Margaret's wielding the crutch like a sword.

"I think we can solve the apartment access issue, especially if we can get help from one of his 'girls.' Let's think the rest through; we're still looking for a way to exterminate him. What health issues do most guys his age worry about?" Susan asked.

"Their tickers and their peckers," Lynn volunteered indelicately.

"I'm guessing that would be high blood pressure, high cholesterol, strokes and erectile disfunction," Susan translated.

Then Karen started to giggle. "I get such a charge out of those Viagra commercials when the voice-over says, 'If your erection lasts longer than four hours, see a doctor.' Girls, if my partner had an erection lasting four hours, I can guarantee I would ask you all over to join the party."

"I'm surprised you could even remember 'the party,'" Lynn said.

"Come on, I had a very active sex life with my third husband, what's his name."

"Bud," the Dames said in unison.

"Yes, Bud. I remember one time when Bud and I were getting frisky. We had this old rescued Tom cat that would sleep at the foot of our bed. He was snoozing away (That's the cat, not Bud. Bud used to fall asleep as soon as he finished.) Anyhow, while Bud was getting all worked up, you know about to climax..."

"Yeah, we know. Go on."

"He kicked the cat out of the way and when he did that, he pulled something. Then he yelled, 'Leg cramp." Well, that was pretty much it for me... and for Bud."

The Dames hooted and snorted. Iced tea squirted from Susan's nose. Margaret and Karen had to leave to use the bathroom. It's a good thing Margaret's apartment had three bathrooms in case a third Dame needed one.

After about five minutes, Margaret hobbled back to the living room and noticed a dejected looking Karen. "Why so sad?"

"Bud left three weeks later." That made the Dames, including Karen, laugh even harder.

"I haven't had such a good workout in years," Lynn said, holding her stomach.

Each time the Dames regained control, something would set them off and they'd squeal again.

"I almost hurt myself ... more," Margaret said. She paused to catch her breath. "Okay, now that we've sort of recovered, can we get back to business? Mr. Miller's meds."

"My ex, the cardiologist, always said that a person should take an aspirin a day to help thin the blood, preventing heart attacks and strokes. I don't think it does a damn thing for ED."

"So maybe we should skip the overdose of Viagra?" Lynn asked.

"I'm thinking more of an 'underdose' or a 'no dose.'" What would happen if Mr. Miller skipped his daily aspirin?"

"Who knows? If he has a bad ticker, he might have a heart attack or stroke out, but we'd have no idea how long it would take. Another wait and see scenario. Maybe we should just call ourselves the Passive Aggressive Dames," Lynn commented.

"All this talk of aspirin makes me remember something

about our first lunch date. When I asked him about his meds, he mentioned taking a daily aspirin."

"And when I was in Laura Ashley hell, I noticed a bottle of aspirin in his guest bathroom. It's clear that he takes a daily aspirin tablet."

"That's it then. We'll take away his aspirin and hope that he strokes out or has a heart attack," Karen said.

"I just hope we live long enough to see the shit 'bite the dust,'" Lynn said. "Anyone for more dessert?"

"Depends," Karen said. The Dames once again burst into uncontrolled laughter.

CHAPTER 12

Let the Good Times Roll!

"Hello, Mr. Miller? This is Margaret, from the Association Board. We met over lemon bars a few weeks ago. I have a favor to ask. I'm currently recovering from a little accident ... Just a few broken bones from a fall... Nothing serious, but I could use some help. Can you come here, say about ten?... No, in the morning... Good, see you soon ... no, Mr. Miller, no need to bring lemon bars." Margaret responded to his "little joke" with a fake laugh. Her next phone call was to Karen to remind her of her offer to chaperone.

Promptly at ten Karen and Margaret received the buffed, polished, hair plugged presumptive "client." He strutted in like a peacock in full feather display, took a look around at Margaret's tasteful contemporary furnishings, so unlike the distasteful kitsch in his own flat, and then broke out laughing.

"What's so funny, Mr. Miller?" Margaret asked.

"This art work, or whatever you call these blotches that a 3-year-old or chimp could've been the artist. What are they supposed to be? I mean art work is supposed to be about something you can recognize, isn't it?"

"Not always. Sometimes art conveys a mood, a feeling, a strong point of view. Sometimes it's just taking a figure or object and stylizing it, like the painting over the fireplace. Abstraction. What does this painting remind you of?"

"Yeah, right, abstraction," he said, laughing again. "Okay,

I'll play your game, girlie. It looks like how I feel after having too many dirty martinis."

Now it was Margaret's turn to laugh. "It's actually an abstraction of a still life with fruit, a bottle of wine, not gin, and a violin."

"You're not going to get me to like it, so don't even try. I like flowers to look like flowers, a person to look like a person, fruit to look like 'fruit.'"

He used air quotes when he said fruit and then he laughed.

Unbelievable, add homophobe to his list of sins. This extermination is going to be such a pleasure. "A house in the country," he continued.

"To look like a house in the country. I get it."

"Now this one I kind of like," Mr. Miller walked over to a watercolor in the dining room. "I can tell that it's a boat on the water. I can see the waves, the sails, the clouds."

"My late husband bought me that watercolor to remind me of our honeymoon," Margaret said. "Every time I look at it I remember the beautiful time we had sailing. Art is supposed to make you feel something," Margaret said, unwilling to give up on the philistine.

"These," he waved his arm around the massive living room, "make me feel something all right." Then he pointed his finger to his mouth, displaying the gag gesture teenagers use when something disgusts them. "They're big, I'll give a that. And colorful. You've got a big place here, girlie, too big for just little ol' you," he said, sidling up to Margaret, totally unaware of Karen sitting on the sectional. Margaret turned away from Mr. Miller and looked at Karen in desperation.

"Yoo-hoo," Karen said with a little wave.

"Hey," Mr. Miller said, "I didn't see you sittin' there. Now I recognize you. You were talking to George at Marco's joint when you nearly fell off the bar stool. George does that to women. We all got a good laugh outta that."

"And didn't my friend, Lynn, throw a little wine at you? You do that to women. My friends got a good laugh outta that."

"Touch-e," Mr. Miller said, mispronouncing *touché*.

"Have a seat, Mr. Miller. May I get you some coffee, some tea, water perhaps?"

"Guess it's too early for a martini," he laughed. "Thanks, girlie, but no thanks. What did I do to deserve all this attention from two such attractive older ladies?" Margaret winced at the word *older*.

"Well, I have a favor to ask." When Margaret said that, he leaned in, suddenly very interested.

"Spill it, girlie. I'm at your service," he said, grinning and displaying those feral eye teeth. *A vampire in a former life?*

"You can see that I'm somewhat incapacitated with this foot and ankle. And since it's my right foot, I can't drive. I'll find out in a few weeks if I have to have surgery. If I do, that will extend my problems for another six weeks. I just thought that one of your girls might be able to help me out. I would pay $25 dollars an hour. She would help with some light housework, but the most important thing would be to drive me around or run some errands. Do you know someone who needs the work, is trustworthy, and a good driver?"

"Yeah, I think I might know just the girl; she's living with me right now and could use the work and the money. Nice kid, screwed up, but aren't they all. Family kicked her outta the house. Me and Marco try to help kids like her, you know." *I bet you do.*

"Tell me about her."

"Medium height, kinda chubby, could drop about ten, you know, pretty when she gets all dolled up."

"Excuse me, Mr. Miller, but Margaret and I want to know what kind of person she is, not what she looks like," Karen said, losing patience with the Plan.

"Sure thing. She's a nice kid. No car accidents that I know of. Nothin' more to say than that. She wouldn't steal, if that's what you're gettin' at," he said, looking around at Margaret's expensive furnishings and accessories as if they were scavenged at garage sales and thrift shops. The only thing cheap in Margaret's apartment was Mr. Miller.

"Right, well, why don't you mention it to her and have her call me if she's interested. What's her name, by the way?"

"It's Tiffany." Margaret nodded in recognition.

"I saw her picture when I brought the lemon bars. You mentioned that she was one of your 'favorites.' Very pretty. I look forward to hearing from her. Thanks so much, Mr. Miller," Margaret stayed seated and put out her hand to shake.

Just then Mr. Miller's phone rang, belting out the old classic, "Come on, Baby, let the good times roll."

"Gotta get this, girls." Mr. Miller walked to the dining room. "Don't panic, girlie, I'll be right there. Sorry, but I have to cut this short. Family emergency." Then he looked at Margaret. "Do I get a hug this time?"

"It hurts her to stand," Karen said, rescuing her friend.

"Of course. No excuses next time, girlie."

"I'll show you out."

"Not necessary. The place ain't that big." He sauntered to the door, stopped, looked around once more and laughed. "Some art," he mumbled.

"Well, that was about as much fun as cramps," Margaret said. "Can you believe that guy?"

"At least we got a lead on Tiffany. Who knows? She might be great. It can't hurt and you do need help with a few things around here. A driver might not be a bad thing at all. If she doesn't work out, we'll think of something else."

Margaret made an effort to get up and groaned.

"Time for a pain pill?"

"Make mine a double," Margaret said.

"I wouldn't mind one myself after spending time with that creep."

"Just be patient, Karen; his days are numbered."

Karen went to the kitchen and came back with two glasses of orange juice and a pain pill for Margaret. Karen lifted her glass for a toast. "To Mr. Miller's demise."

"To Mr. Miller's demise," Margaret said, clinking Karen's glass.

"'Come on, baby, let the good times roll,'" Karen said and they both burst into laughter.

CHAPTER 13

Breakfast with Tiffany

Two days later Margaret got a phone call from Tiffany, Mr. Miller's protege. They scheduled a breakfast meeting for the following morning.

When the doorbell rang, Margaret limped to answer it, surprised to find both Mr. Miller and Tiffany.

"Come on in, Tiffany." She stared at Mr. Miller. "I wasn't expecting you."

"Just wanted to help with the introductions. Not going to stay. Tiff here, is a little shy meeting people for the first time."

"Not so much these days, Bob. I'm not that scared teenager any more. Besides she doesn't look dangerous."

Margaret put out her hand to Tiffany. "Hi, I'm Margaret and you're right: I'm not dangerous, at least most days," Margaret said, laughing.

"Figured. You can go now, Bob," Tiffany said to Bob, who just stood there, not taking the hint.

"I'll take it from here, Mr. Miller."

Bob looked at Tiffany. "Call if you need anything, Tiff. Otherwise, I'll see you for dinner tonight at Marco's. Got some pals I'd like you to meet."

"Thanks, Bob," Tiffany said, rolling her eyes at Bob's exit line. "Excuse Bob; he's overly protective."

Controlling is more like it. He's probably setting her up for a few "dates." Margaret decided to keep her opinions to herself, at least for the time being. She didn't want to spook her.

Tiffany walked around Margaret's living room, feasting on the original art and clean, uncluttered surroundings. There was nary a flower in sight except for the bouquet of lilies on Margaret's dining room table. She reminded Margaret of Lynn at a dessert buffet, sizing up the offerings before filling her plate to overflowing. When she came to the abstract painting above the fireplace, she smiled. "Beautiful... Kandinsky meets Cezanne... more Kandinsky I'd say."

"I do believe you're right." *How did she become interested in art?*

As if Tiffany could read Margaret's mind, "Most people think I'm just a dumb kid Bob took under his wing and are surprised when I show an interest in art, music, literature, theatre."

She anticipated my reaction — bright, intuitive woman. Caught in the act of stereotyping, Margaret hung her head as an apology.

"No need to be embarrassed. Happens all the time. So to answer the question you didn't ask ... When I was a kid and had some extra time, I'd go to the Minneapolis Institute of Art on Thursdays when it was free. I'd just hang out for hours, but I just kept coming back to Kandinsky. He became my favorite artist. A Russian rebel, I liked that." Margaret remembered Mr. Miller's comments about Tiffany's teenage years when she was kicked out of her home.

"I hope to go to college eventually and study art history. I went to cosmetology school, but I didn't really like it that much. I even tried working in a salon, but I didn't like that much either. I'm currently at loose ends." *She's beginning to open up. This might work.*

"Come on into the kitchen and meet Lynn who's helping me with breakfast. She's made an egg bake; we have fresh fruit and croissants as well with a delicious cheesecake for dessert, compliments of our very own gourmet restaurant."

"I'm amazed at the amenities of this place. No way could I ever afford to live here if it weren't for Bob. But I'd be happier if I could have my own place maybe one of those small apartments across from the Institute of Arts. If I could only make enough money... I've been trying to save up. This job will definitely help."

This girl's a surprise—not at all what I expected. Her glamorous picture was certainly deceptive. That must have been Bob's doing, wanting her to look cheap instead of naturally beautiful like she is. And he said she needed to lose about ten pounds. What a jerk!

The conversation around the breakfast table was light, unforced, natural. The women discussed food, movies, books, TV shows, fashion, vacations, like women do when getting acquainted. Tiff, as she preferred being called, was comfortable with the questions and seemed to be enjoying herself until Lynn asked about how she came to be living with Bob. Then the light, open, fun banter stopped like a car braking for a wild animal and Tiff became very tense, almost frightened.

"Sorry, I didn't mean to pry, but it is rather an unusual situation. He isn't a relative after all," Lynn said in an attempt to apologize. She got up to clear the dishes.

"Let me help," Tiff said. "It's just hard to talk about that time of my life." She helped rinse the dishes and load the dishwasher.

"I understand," Lynn said.

"Thanks, you two. Lynn, the breakfast was delicious. If you don't mind, I think I will put my leg up and relax while you two work away. I'll be so glad when I can get back to being independent. When you're done, come in the living room and we can discuss the job."

Margaret decided to let the two women have some time to get acquainted. Besides she needed time to process the plan a bit more. Maybe Lynn could get some additional information. She limped back into the living room and got comfortable in her leather chair. Her pain lessened considerably when her foot was elevated. She closed her eyes and was soon sleeping.

About a half hour later, the women returned to the living room. Margaret quickly awakened.

"I'll let you two talk jobs. I've gotta go. The grandkids are coming later for a swim."

"Thanks again, Lynn."

"I'll stop by this afternoon to see if you need anything."

* * *

"Well, what did you two decide?" Lynn asked.

"She'll start by working three half days a week. I'll have her drive me to the doctor's and run some errands. I think it might take awhile to get her to open up. Did you have any luck?"

"Actually, I did get to know her a bit while we were cleaning up in the kitchen. It's too bad that everyone had to buy dishwashers; they might be responsible for the disintegration of the American family. I think I should write an oped piece about that very thing. When I was a girl, my sibs and I did the dishes, well mostly we screwed around, but the dishes got done and we had fun doing them. I remember one time ... " *Geriatric ADD strikes again.*

"Lynn, what did you learn about Tiff? I've heard the story about how your mom would make you re-wash the dishes if you missed anything a million times. I want to know about Tiff."

"Sorry for just being me," Lynn said ready to start an argument. She apparently thought better of it because she answered Margaret's question.

"Tiff told me about how she ran away from home because she got caught smoking a joint in the girls' lav at her high school and her parents 'freaked' and kicked her out of the house. She ended up on the streets and that's where she met Bob."

"You mean she was a hooker?" Margaret asked, thinking the worst.

BARBARA GRENGS

"She didn't actually admit to that, but I think it's a real possibility."

"I wonder if Bob pimped her out or whatever the term is. Or if he still is. He mentioned that at dinner tonight she was meeting a few of his pals. Remember Susan found out some info about him early on in our investigation. Wasn't he arrested for pimping or was it for being a john? I forget." Margaret found that the pain pills made her mind a bit fuzzy.

"Probably both. Hey, wait a minute. You mentioned Bob was setting Tiff up to meet some of his pals; maybe we should all go to dinner at Marco's tonight to check it out. If Tiff gets uncomfortable, she could always join us. Do you think you're up for a little field trip? I could always go for their mushroom ravioli."

"Maybe if I take nap and another pain pill. It might fun to get out."

"I'll check with Karen and Susan to see if they have plans, and if not, make a reservation for seven."

"That might just work out," Margaret said.

"Any cheesecake left?" Lynn didn't wait for an answer, but went directly to the kitchen and helped herself to breakfast leftovers and one of Margaret's pain killers which gave her a welcome buzz. She deserved it after spending a few hours watching the grandkids swim.

"Please bring me a pain pill and some juice while you're out there."

"Sure thing."

CHAPTER 14

Dollars to Donuts It's E-Mail Love

The day of Margaret's accident Susan recalled her own and threw herself one hell of a pity party by drinking a whole bottle of her favorite red blend and reading old love letters and news clippings of the accident. Then she broke the single woman's cardinal rule: Do not drink and e-mail old flames. Now why would she want to e-mail such a loser other than she was drunk, lonely and a bit bored.

Boredom had always been a problem for Susan because she was so bright and curious. Elementary school was way too easy for her, even after being placed in many of the advanced reading groups: "blue bird," (1st grade) "cardinal" (second grade) more birds until sixth grade when her teacher switched from biology to mythology and called the advanced group "Athena" and the slow group "Ares." Susan intuitively knew, even at the young age of eleven, that the gender delineation was accurate.

Sixth grade was the year she learned to love Greek mythology and to adore reading. She subsequently prayed to Athena to send her a teacher who would just leave her alone so she could finally read whatever she wanted. Her prayer was finally answered when Susan's 11th grade English teacher said, "Just go to the library for an hour, read your favorite authors, and then show me what you've learned. We'll call it even." So Susan went and read all she could about and by Willa Cather, Emily Dickinson, Sarah Orne Jewett, Kate Chopin, and Charlotte Perkins Gilman. Bam! A Feminist/English major was born. Susan was no longer bored.

In college Susan continued her feminist leanings and went on to "burn her bra" with other political activists. Fortunately for her and her breasts, she came to her senses somewhere in the mid '70s and became more interested in computers and less interested in male bashing.

After attending a job fair in Minneapolis, Susan was hired by Control Data and stayed with them for over twenty years until she made her fortune designing computer software games for children, ironic because Susan didn't really like children, but she did remember being bored as a kid.

Pre-accident Susan was relatively attractive and well-groomed at five-six, one hundred thirty pounds, with dark brown naturally curly hair, and straight white teeth. Not fashion-obsessed like some of her friends, she dressed modestly and with classic styles that didn't change each year. Though basically an introvert, she was at least social enough to join a few friends for drinks at the local watering hole on Friday afternoons. On that fateful day when she was destined to meet Mr. Right, she wore a green and white print sundress short enough to show off her legs, but not so short that she looked like she was on the make. It was at one of these TGIF celebrations that she first met Steve, an up-and-coming Minneapolis architect. It was not love at first sight.

Susan and her work friends were sitting at a large round table at Tailgate Sports Bar having wine and appetizers, enjoying Happy Hour, when she noticed this tall handsome man standing at the bar staring at her. Unused to being stared at, Susan tried to ignore him, but every time she looked up, there he was, drinking his beer and staring. It was disturbing, so she decided to do something about it and confront his rudeness. On the pretense of using the rest room, she excused herself and went directly to the bar.

On the way there, she kept saying to herself, "I am a fifty-three-year-old, strong, financially independent woman. I own my own home and have a sizable 401K and stock portfolio. I don't have to put up with this shit." Susan was a firm believer in positive self talk.

Once she got there, however, face to face with this attractive man, all that self-talk went out the window and she simply said, "What are you drinking?" She had intended to say, "What's your problem?"

"Excuse me?" he said, still staring off in the direction of her table. It was then she realized he was watching the golf match on the TV, not staring at her at all.

"Nothing. I was just on my way to the rest room." *He probably didn't hear me with the noise in here.*

"Summit Pale Ale." Tall Handsome Man took a drink.

"Can't stand beer myself. Even on a hot day. Now if you'll excuse me."

"I believe you came here to say something to me and I don't think it was 'What are you drinking?'"

"What makes you think that?"

"I'll bet you dollars to donuts you thought I was staring at you and when you realized I was watching golf and not you, you got nervous and changed your mind," he said, laughing.

"Who says 'dollars to donuts' anyway? What does that even mean?"

"It was one of my granny's favorite sayings. I think it sounds pleasantly alliterative, kind of like the Brits saying 'a pound to a penny.' It means short odds, a certainty. I kind of like the sound of it."

"You're right. I did think you were staring at me. I was intending to call you on your rudeness."

"And why didn't you?"

"I'm not sure."

"Yes, you are. You became flummoxed when you got close and blurted out the first thing that came to you." *Flummoxed, you've got to be kidding me. Who is this guy anyway?*

"Why, you arrogant prick. How's that for blurting? Now excuse me; I have to use the ladies' room." Susan stomped off and tried to figure out exactly how she was going to return to her table without walking past him. *'Flummoxed' my ass.* She didn't have to worry because he was gone when she rejoined her pals.

The next few Fridays Susan looked for him, but he never showed. She was embarrassed because she found herself dressing slightly less casually for Casual Fridays and the next Friday even tried a Summit Pale Ale. It was quite refreshing.

"Thought you didn't like beer," he said, coming up behind her and tapping her on the shoulder. Susan turned around surprised to see Tall Handsome Man dressed in a blue dress shirt that matched his eyes, sleeves rolled up, no tie, and jeans. He smiled, showing her his dimples. She was a sucker for dimples.

Since Susan wasn't known to do much dating, a good-looking guy tapping her on the shoulder was a definite "show stopper," and the boisterous banter at her table came to a sudden halt. The shoulder tap left Susan speechless as well.

"Mind if I join you? I was here a few weeks ago at the bar, stared at this woman, and she gave me hell for my rudeness. I believe the exact phrase used was 'arrogant prick.'"

By this time, Susan was blushing.

Her pals laughed at her embarrassment and her language. Maggie, her best friend from work, said, "That's our Susan. We love her anyway."

"Nice to meet you, Susan. My name is Steve," Steve held out his hand. She felt her stomach flip a bit. That handshake sealed the deal.

Steve joined the gang from work and from then on Susan and Steve were a couple.

Until the accident when everything changed.

* * *

Post accident Susan dressed directly from the dryer, showered every three or four days, wore glasses because she was too lazy to put in her contacts, and drank too much. Case in point: drunken e-mail. Once she pressed *send*, she became e-mail obsessed, checking for a message from Steve every few hours. This pathetic behavior reminded her of her teen-age years when she sat waiting by the phone for her crush *du jour* to call. And then, while researching Mr. Miller's pals, she got the notification that she had mail:

Dear Susan,

I was surprised and delighted to hear from you after all this time. I've thought about you often. After reading the article in Minnesota Monthly *magazine, I knew about your successful career and your beautiful apartment — very impressive layout, by the way — but I wondered if you were happy.*

I know that breaking off our engagement was cowardly and I sincerely apologize. Maybe we can be friends?

Steve

Dear Steve,

Thanks for responding. I've been curious about you as well. Obviously I know about your award, your impressive career and your marriage. Sorry that didn't work out.

I've made three very good friends where I live and I'm happy with my occasional consulting jobs and my apartment, though I sometimes wish my life had taken a more traditional path. Maybe I should get a dog? And yes, I think we can be friends.

Susan

Dear Susan,

I'm so happy that you feel we can be friends. I tried dating after the divorce, but hated all the pretense and game playing.

You were far from pretentious and definitely didn't like dating games, but if I remember correctly you played a mean game of poker and beat my ass in Scrabble a few times. You always challenged me to be a better person. I always felt I could trust you. I can't say that about any other woman I've known, except my granny, of course.

You mentioned a dog; I have two rescue mutts who keep me walking and laughing. Dogs are amazing creatures: trusting, loving, and loyal. Much better company than my ex! I even take them to work with me every day. My clients seem more relaxed when Mutt and Jeff are around. Dumb names, I know.

I'm available for dog adoption counseling if you're interested.

    Steve

Dear Steve,

"Dollars to donuts" I remember all those sayings you used from your beloved granny. I used to get a kick out of her quotes that became your quotes and started using a few of them myself. I found myself saying "the world is going to hell in a hand basket" just yesterday. Mutt and Jeff—are you kidding me?

No surprise coming from a man who named his firm Gilbert and Sullivan. What happened, Steve, to the wildly creative guy I knew? The one who surprised me with his old worn, leather briefcase for my birthday. I still have it, by the way, sitting in my bedroom filled with magazines.

What kind of dog would you recommend for me? We do have a dog walker available in my building, but I think I could handle one on my own. My motorized wheelchair could give the pooch quite the workout. Our community has beautiful walking paths and gardens.

Please advise,

Susan

Dear Susan,

So glad Granny is alive and well in our use of language. As for my firm's name—how could I not make the joke first? I've found with clients it's a real ice breaker. Yum Yum.

Now for dogs—I like mutts. I've sent you pictures of the boys so you can see why the Mutt and Jeff names fit. Mutts seem to be healthier than some of the purebreds. Mutt is a border collie mix which means he's smarter than most people and Jeff is a basset-corgi combo and a real clown. I could go on and on about the "kids." I think you should do what you do best: get online and research. Try rescues first; so many dogs need good homes; you'd be a great doggy "mom."

My business partner is a great guy and has been very easy to work with. You'd like him; he's *direct, funny, and "wildly creative." I'm the practical one (can you believe it?) and Rick is the risk taker. We make a good team. If you're interested you can see some of our work on our website.*

I look forward to our daily and nightly chats. You've always been a terrific friend.

Thanks for giving me a second chance. Ready for a VC?

Steve

Dear Steve,

I did check out your website and you guys are fabulous. I loved the house overlooking the lake — the colors, the use of glass and rock, the contemporary furnishings alongside antiques. Beautiful, practical, ecologically responsible.

I took your advice about a dog and found myself a funny looking thing at the Humane Society. A dalmatian, Doberman, pit bull, shepherd, German short hair — who knows. She's a medium sized dog — about forty-five pounds, about three years old and a love. Her owner gave her up when she had to move. As soon as I saw her polka dot tail, I was a goner. And she has these polka dot eyebrows that move separately — weird but adorable. They let me take her for a walk and she wasn't afraid of the wheelchair at all. In fact, she took to it "like a duck to water," as my granny used to say.

I've hired Bruce, the dog walker, to take her out first thing in the morning for a long walk. Then I take her in the afternoon, if the weather cooperates, and Bruce returns around ten for last potty call. So far it's worked well — no accidents. And she sleeps like a baby, snores like a man, and eats like my friend Lynn who is constantly dieting. All the exercise should keep her in good shape.

As for a VC, I'll have to have a glass of wine first. Let me know what time works for you.

Susan

Dear Susan,

Me too. See you at nine Wednesday. Hope that's not too late.

I want to see the pooch. You too, of course. What did you name her by the way? Spot?

Steve

Dear Steve,

Dot.

Susan

Dear Susan,

Figures.

Steve

CHAPTER 15

Dinner with the Dames

"Susan, you look fabulous! I love what you've done with your hair!" Margaret was her usual positive self. She needed Karen's help to get into Susan's specially equipped van, but she managed. "I'll be so glad when I can ditch these crutches."

"Thanks, I needed a change, and then the beautician talked me into getting it colored as well as cut. It's close to my natural color without the gray. It took me awhile to get used to it, but now I like it. It's much easier to take care of and it doesn't take forever to dry."

"It's very becoming and you look years younger and considerably more rested," Lynn said from the back seat.

"Do you think I should color my gray?" Karen said, patting her short gray hair. "I tried Susan's color in my forties, but I did it myself. All I remember is having dark brown pillow cases and brown dandruff. My third husband, (what's his name?), made fun of me."

"Bud; it's Bud," the Dames said in unison.

"I know. I just like hearing you yell his name."

In no time at all Susan pulled into Costello's crowded parking lot. With her handicapped license plate, she always got a prime spot close to the entrance, a good thing, considering Margaret and her crutches.

"I love driving with you, Susan, 'cause there are never any parking hassles," Lynn said.

"It's my pleasure to be handicapped," Susan said as the wheelchair lift lowered her to the pavement. Lynn helped Margaret out of the van.

"Our reservations are for seven. I'm kind of taking a chance here on the timing. It's possible Bob and Tiffany's 'date' will be at a later time, but I figured the men she's probably meeting are old retirees and prefer to eat early," Margaret said.

"That's one advantage to 'servicing' the elderly. You'd get home early," Karen said, laughing.

"Poor Tiff," Margaret said.

"Another Dames adventure. Don't you just love it?" Lynn said, eager to have her mushroom ravioli and few glasses of wine. Good food always made her giddy.

They were greeted by a dapper young man wearing a white open-collared shirt, tight black dress pants and hot pink suspenders. "This way, Ladies." Margaret and Susan followed him to their table with Lynn and Karen close behind.

"My, isn't he cute? I just love young guys' butts," Lynn said, staring.

"You should see Vince, the bartender," Karen whispered.

"You can remember Vince's name, but not your third husband. You are so weird."

"My third husband wasn't all that cute and his butt was saggy."

"Hopefully you won't fall off the bar stool and start speaking French, like the last time you were here," Lynn said.

"I didn't fall. I was caught by the gorgeous man with the dimples, the one who looked like George Clooney. As for the French ... I can make no promises."

After seating all the ladies, Cute Greeter Guy said, "Your waiter will be with you in a moment. May I get you a beverage from the bar?"

"*Certainement,*" Karen said, winking at Lynn. "We'll take

a bottle of white and a bottle of red. What would you recommend?"

The bar side of the restaurant was filled with young millennials ready to party. Since it was so hot, there were only a few brave souls on the patio which made it easier for the Dames to scope out the joint. The older crowd was seated in the main dining room where it was much quieter and more relaxing. Margaret hoped that was where they'd find Tiffany, Bob, and the "boys."

When the waiter brought the wine and poured glasses for everyone, Susan proposed a toast. "To friendship, wine, and love," Susan said, raising her glass. The Dames raised their eyebrows. Susan never talked about love.

"I noticed your new blouse, Susan. You also have a new hairdo and you just mentioned love in your toast. Is there something you want to tell us, Dear?" Lynn said in her fake grandma voice.

"Spill the beans, girlie, to use Mr. Miller's demeaning label," Karen said.

And for the next ten minutes Susan "spilled the beans." The Dames were momentarily stunned into silence, all of them remembering their past loves and romances.

"Are you lovely ladies ready to order?" The Dames were jolted back to the present.

"Can you give us just a few more minutes. There are so many delicious choices," Margaret said.

"There certainly are," Karen said, looking at Lynn and grinning.

"Maybe we should order before we start interrogating Susan."

They were in the middle of the salad course and the interrogation, when Lynn spied Mr. Miller with a movie star glamorous woman on his arm. They were headed out to the patio.

"Oh, my god, look at Mr. Miller's babe!" Lynn exclaimed, salad dressing on her chin. She went so far as to point.

"Keep your voice down and don't point. We don't want them to see us, at least not yet," Margaret said.

Mr. Miller's dark-haired "babe" was tall and voluptuous, filling out her black cocktail dress to the max.

"Look at those fuck me shoes," Lynn said, still staring open-mouthed. "How does she walk in those? Those sandals must have four inch heels."

"That 'babe' is our Tiffany," Margaret said. "I can't believe the transformation."

"She certainly looks the part of high-priced escort," Karen said, just as the entrees were delivered. "So what do we do now?"

"Nothing. We're here to watch and enjoy this fine dinner," Margaret said. And that's just what they did until Bob's pals showed up.

About half way through their *tiramisu* and coffee, two elderly gentlemen walked out on the patio to join Mr. Miller and Tiffany.

Lynn, who had the best vantage point for spying, gave a detailed account of what was happening on the patio. She'd also had three small glasses of white wine.

"Mr. Miller is introducing Tiff to the two men. The fat one with the Trump comb-over and the blue bulbous nose is taking Tiff's hand and kissing it." Lynn made an exaggerated smooching sound. The Dames grimaced. "Now the other man, the bald one wearing the polka dot bow tie, is asking Tiff to turn around like she's modeling her cocktail dress. Is he doing what I think he's doing?"

"Afraid so. I fear Tiff might not be getting home early after all. It's disgusting, that's what it is," Karen said.

"Maybe we should try to rescue her before it goes any farther," Susan said.

"I don't think so. She might take care of it herself. Let's wait it out," Margaret said. "We don't want to cause her any additional pain. Bob might take it out on her."

"Oh, oh, now Fat Guy is taking a look. She's turning around again. Tiff doesn't seem to be upset; she's laughing.

Mr. Miller just called the waiter over and is talking to him. Maybe their table is ready or they're ordering drinks. Speaking of which... " She motioned for the bottle.

"No more for you," Karen said, pouring the last of the white into her own glass.

"They're coming back inside. Now what should we do?" Lynn was getting a little nervous.

"Finish our desserts. It seems Tiff is doing just fine," Margaret said. "In fact, Tiff just waved at me." The Dames turned as one and stared; Tiff waved at them too.

"Well, I never. She's not embarrassed in the least," Karen said as she poured herself more coffee. "Didn't you say she wanted to go to college for a degree in Art History? That's one way to pay for your education. Lynn, more coffee?"

"No thanks. If I drink coffee before bed, I won't sleep a wink. I bet the boys won't be doing much sleeping either."

"Are you kidding me? One round each and they'll be out like a light. Dollars to donuts she'll be back in her hideous bedroom at Bob's before midnight. If we want to stage a rescue, we should save her from bad decorating," Margaret said.

Hearing "Dollars to donuts," Susan laughed. *Now what are the chances of that?*

"Don't laugh. You haven't seen Mr. Miller's apartment," Margaret said.

"More coffee, Susan?"

"No thanks, I'm driving."

CHAPTER 16

The Morning After or The Hair of the Dog

"Have you seen Susan walking her dog? What's that about anyway? First the new hair-do, then the clothes, then the dog. I get the hair and clothes because of renewing her friendship or whatever with Steve, but a dog? Susan is like a whole new person," Lynn said to Karen during their morning chat over coffee.

"Why do you care?" Karen said.

"Here are your two aspirin, Crabby Pants."

"Thanks. I shouldn't have had red wine last night; it gives me a headache." She rubbed her temples and then downed the aspirin with her orange juice.

"That's why I was drinking white."

"Point taken."

"I would get it if she got a cat or two; they're much lower maintenance and you don't have to walk them. You can even leave them overnight without worrying about them peeing or pooping all over." Just as she said that Missy Pissy jumped on her lap.

"And that's why your apartment stinks of cat pee," Karen said.

"Missy is sixteen and has issues."

"All your cats have 'issues.'"

"It doesn't stink too bad, does it?"

"Don't worry about it. We're used to it. I like the new Susan; she's much happier and I say if a dog makes you happy, get a dog. Dottie is kind of cute in a funky way. I love her expressive eyebrows. Besides getting out is good for Susan; she's been virtually housebound for years. I was beginning to think she might be ... what's that phobia?"

"Agoraphobia. See the old brain is still working."

"Way to go, Lynn."

"I don't think she's agoraphobic. It just takes so much effort to go out that she says, 'to hell with it' and stays in."

"Good thing she has Bruce to help. He's walking Dottie twice a day: morning and night. I'd even be willing to help if the weather was bad."

"You're a good friend." Karen took her cup and glass into the kitchen. "And thanks for the coffee, juice, aspirin and drinking advice. I think I'll lie down before the meeting this afternoon."

* * *

When the Dames got to Margaret's apartment, she had displayed three purses on the dining room table: a blue canvas shoulder bag, a coffee-colored shoulder tote, and a funky orange and cream travel bag, all designer knock-offs.

Lynn went straight to the kitchen to check on refreshments. She came back munching on a chocolate covered strawberry.

"What's with the cute purses?" Susan said as she wheeled into the living room with Dottie at her side. At the sight of the dog, the Dames gasped, shocked that Susan might sully Margaret's pristine apartment with dog hair.

"Don't worry about Dottie; she's well-behaved, except she does shed."

"The hair of the dog. I love it. Anyone for a Bloody Mary?" Lynn said, laughing.

"I get a headache just thinking about it. No thanks."

"Dottie's fine. I love dogs, as long as they belong to someone else. Tiff is coming tomorrow and she can vacuum. I'm pleased to meet your beautiful companion. Come here,

Sweetie." Dottie wagged her tail, sniffed Margaret's hand and boot, then sat docilely at Margaret's feet. She seemed to sense Margaret's injury.

"If you remember our last meeting, we decided a less aggressive approach to Mr. Miller would be prudent. We know he takes a daily aspirin, and we know he's concerned about his heart. So, if we're patient and take away his aspirin, he might just have a heart attack or a stroke. Lucky for us, not so lucky for him. Now about the purses. Since Tiff has been helping me, I've noticed she uses three different purses for everyday use. When I admired them, she told me she ordered them online and gave me the site. So I ordered the same three purses."

"Brilliant!" Susan said.

"I'm not following," Lynn said.

"The purse—wasn't that my idea? I thought we could get into her purse, steal the keys, and make copies and you guys all laughed at me."

"You're right, Karen. Your idea got me thinking about how to get the keys. I think the purse switch might give us more time to execute the plan and be less suspicious. This way we might not have to make a copy of Mr. Miller's apartment key."

"As long as I get some credit for this." The Dames made mock bows in Karen's direction until she laughed.

"This is how I see the plan," said Susan. "Correct me, Margaret, if I'm wrong. You'll have each of the purses filled with your stuff and then before Tiff goes to run errands for you, you'll switch purses, allowing us to get her keys, run up to Mr. Miller's apartment and exchange the real aspirin for the fake. Just be sure to tell us which purse she's using the day of the switch."

"What if she goes to use something in her purse like her phone or her wallet and realizes the purse isn't hers?" Karen asked.

"I suppose that's always a possibility, but I've noticed when we run errands she focuses on my needs not hers. She even turns off her phone so she's not distracted. She'll have my car keys and, hopefully, won't look in her purse, but if she does, I'll have to 'fess up and say that I liked her purse so much I bought one myself. I'll play the forgetful old lady card on pain meds who mixed up the purses by mistake," Margaret said.

"That might work," Karen conceded.

Lynn raised her hand.

"Yes, Lynn?" Margaret called on her like she was the teacher and Lynn a wiggly seventh grader.

"Won't we need to count the aspirin to know how many to replace and get an idea about when he'll need to buy more?"

"Good point, Lynn. I think all we'll have to do is guess the number based on the number of pills originally in the bottle. If the bottle holds 100 pills, half a bottle is 50, etc.. That should be close enough," Susan said.

"How will you distract Tiff to make the switch?" Karen asked. "We need to buy some extra time because Margaret can't move very fast."

"And what about Mr. Miller? We'll need to make sure he's gone. We wouldn't want to be surprised in the midst of the exchange. And what are we going to use for fake aspirin?"

"All excellent questions and that's where I'll need your help," Margaret said. "Lynn, would you please get the whiteboard from the hall storage closet? Let's brainstorm."

Distract Tiff

1. Someone besides Margaret needs to distract her

2. A problem with Dottie?

"What about my cats? Why is it always about the dog?"

3. A problem with Lynn's cats?

"We won't need to distract her for long; the switch will only take about five minutes," Susan said.

"Remember, I can't move very fast so the three purses will have to be close by, but not in a place where Tiff will see them."

4. One of us could call with a fake medical emergency.

5. One of us could use our "manly" voice and demand an emergency booty call.

The Dames all hooted at the booty.

After some discussion, they decided that Susan would be the most likely to need help and Dottie was a perfect distraction.

"Like she might need to go out because she ate something and her tummy was upset. That might work," Susan said. "I'll think of a plausible scenario."

Mr. Miller's schedule:

1. Weasel it out of Tiff.

2. Weekly lunch with frat brothers. Find out which day.

"Maybe one of us could ask at Costello's bar?" Karen said, with a gleam in her eye.

"You just want to talk with George again or that cute bartender, Vince."

3. Weasel it out of Mr. Miller.

"We could maybe ask Mr. Miller for dinner and ask him which days don't work for him," Lynn said, "but then we might actually have to have him for dinner."

4. Stalk Mr. Miller.

"It seems our best chance would be to ask the bartender or get Tiff to tell us what she knows. Margaret, why don't you try Tiff first? And then we could hit up the bartender," Susan said. "Anything to avoid actually sitting down and having dinner with his assholiness."

Fake aspirin:

1. Check our medicine cabinets for aspirin look-alikes.

2. Research online for placebos.

"Susan, you do the online research and we'll all check our non-prescription drugs for anything that looks like aspirin."

"So what do we do first?" Karen asked.

"I think we can all check our medicine cabinets. I'll work on Tiff when she comes to help tomorrow. We'll have lunch, maybe do some bonding and talk about things, like her life and the choices she's made. I might be able to help. And I might get lucky to find out something about Mr. Miller's schedule.

"In the meantime, let's have some dessert and find out the juicy details about Susan's new 'friend,' and I don't mean Dottie. We need to take a break from Mr. Miller," Margaret said. The Dames agreed.

"It's nummy strawberry shortcake," said Lynn.

Dottie barked just once.

"She either likes strawberry shortcake or she needs to go potty," Susan said with a grin.

Margaret looked horrified.

"Just kidding. She went right before we got here."

Dottie sat at Margaret's feet, put her head in her lap, and gave her the Pathetic Dog Stare. It was too much for Margaret, so she gave Dottie a tiny taste of the cake with whipped cream. "You're right, Lynn. It's always about the dog."

CHAPTER 17

Romance is in the Air.

Margaret hired Tiff three days a week to do light housework, run errands and take her to the doctor. If she had to have surgery, she would need even more help. She hoped that the regular contact with Tiff would engender trust and thereby give her some valuable information to make this "extermination" happen sooner rather than later.

Two days after their last meeting, Margaret called the Dames and invited them for cheese and wine to update them on info gathered from Tiff, her current medical condition and also to pick their brains about aspirin substitutes. Then there was the gossip, of course.

Exactly at five the Dames and Dottie swarmed Margaret's apartment like mosquitos at dusk. It was a good thing Margaret was seated in her chair with her leg up because Dottie ran right to her and gave her a big, slobbery kiss on the cheek. If she had been standing, she might have broken something else.

"I love you too," Margaret said, cuddling the friendly beast.

"Looks like you've made a pal for life," Susan said, laughing.

"I'm pumped and ready to get this show on the road!" Lynn yelled as she barged in. Karen followed with a big bouquet of farmer's market flowers for Margaret, already arranged and in a vase.

"I want the vase back," Karen said. Karen always wanted the vases back and that request was easily honored because the vases were ugly. Karen had a definite way with ugly. Just consider all those too small sweaters made from garage sale yarn.

"The flowers are absolutely beautiful, Karen. Tiff just threw away Susan's lily bouquet today. They lasted well over a week."

"These probably won't last that long, but you should get four or five days out of them, at least. I went to the farmer's market in St. Luke's parking lot and couldn't resist. Ladies, the vegetables were absolutely beautiful, the smells, the sounds, the tastes... " Karen, a farmer's market junky, was almost orgasmic in her enthusiasm.

"Well, I went to Trader Joe's, not exactly a farmer's market, to get cheese and ended up buying six bottles of Honeymoon white wine, a recommendation from a customer. I tried a bottle last night and it's not bad. The wine is in the cooler, the cheese platter and the glasses are on the counter. Ladies, 'let the good times roll!'"

"Should we bring the food to the living room coffee table?" Lynn yelled from the kitchen.

"I wouldn't if I were you. I have a counter surfer here with Miss Dottie. She's eaten several sandwiches and a piece of salmon off my kitchen counter. I now push everything back as far as I can."

"Good to know," Lynn said. "I'll bring the chocolate covered strawberries and put them on the mantle. The wine can go on the coffee table unless, of course, Dot's a drinker. If we need seconds or thirds of the cheese and crackers, we can get them ourselves. I don't know about you, but I'm counting this as today's exercise."

Once everyone had a glass of wine and snacks, Margaret called the "meeting" to order.

"I have some news," Margaret said. "Tiffany told me Bob's luncheon meeting at Costello's happens on Thursdays at 11:30 a.m., so that's one problem solved."

"Good. That was easy. We can check that off our list," Susan said. "Do we need to get the whiteboard and check things off?"

"I erased everything in case Tiff might see it. We should be able to remember everything. We're not that old and senile, except for Lynn who keeps forgetting Bud's name."

"Who's Bud?" Lynn asked. The Dames laughed much to Lynn's delight.

"Did Tiff say anything about seeing us at Costello's? Was she embarrassed? Ashamed?" Karen asked, adjusting her ill-fitting cardigan.

"Not in the least. Remember she waved at all of us. She said she had just bought that cocktail dress and was showing it off to the 'old coots,' her words. The comb-over, blue nosed coot had given her the money to buy a new dress for her twenty-second birthday which they were apparently celebrating. It appears that it was an innocent gathering."

"You're not having second thoughts are you?" Susan asked.

"No, not at all. In this particular case, I think it was simply a birthday party. Once I knew it was her birthday, I felt a little gift was in order, so I gave her a birthday bonus since she's trying to save for college and her own apartment." Margaret's "little gifts" were legendary. Last year each of the Dames got $500 Pamper Yourself Spa gift certificates for their birthdays. "We should move ahead as planned. What did you find out about aspirin substitutes?"

"When I was cleaning out my medicine cabinet, I found a generic antacid tablet, that was white and about the size of an aspirin tablet. That might work," Karen said.

"I found a homeopathic sleep med that was white and the same size. Just think, he might fall asleep at the wheel and have an accident. We wouldn't have to wait around for him to stroke out or have a heart attack," Lynn suggested.

"But what if Tiff took two aspirin for a headache and ended up falling asleep at the wheel while driving Margaret? We can't guarantee Mr. Miller will be the only one using the aspirin," Susan said.

"And what if he hurts or kills someone else in that accident?" Karen said.

"My bad." Lynn hung her head, embarrassed because it was a dumb idea. "I guess we can dump the sleep med as a possibility."

"Susan, what did you find out about placebos?" Margaret asked.

"I got online and found there are sugar placebos you can buy that look very much like aspirin. I ordered a bottle from Amazon that should be arriving in the next few days so we can actually see what they look like. I think we should hold off on this decision until I get the pills."

"Why would anyone buy sugar pills when you can have a chocolate-coated strawberry?" Lynn, now recovered, asked, munching on her third.

"Looks like item two is taken care of. We know that Mr. Miller has lunch out on Thursdays. We've tabled item three, waiting for the placebos to arrive. Now for one: How to distract Tiff? Remember I need adequate time to get the purse. I'm really slow on the crutches."

"I would like to volunteer Dottie and myself for that job. I will call Margaret on a Thursday and ask if Tiff can take Dottie outside to go potty around eleven-thirty, because I don't feel well. That will give you plenty of time to switch purses. Then you two can go run an errand, maybe go to the bank, something that lasts about an hour or slightly less. Try to keep her busy accommodating your needs so she doesn't need her purse. You can monitor the time and adjust your plans as needed. That will give Lynn and Karen enough time to search the apartment and make the placebo/aspirin switch. Mr. Miller's lunch should last at least an hour and a half with their having drinks and food. Does that make sense?"

"As long as Mr. Miller doesn't cut his lunch short. If he does, we're screwed," Karen said.

"Let's just hope he has a couple of dirty martinis and lots of spaghetti and meatballs," Lynn said.

"I can be sitting in the lobby and if Mr. Miller shows up early, I'll give you a call. That should help ease your anxiety a bit. Just remember to bring your cell phone, not like the mushroom debacle," Susan said.

"Thanks. Good idea. I'm getting more wine and cheese. Anybody else interested?" Lynn went to the kitchen, fixed a small plate of snacks for Margaret and refilled her glass, then loaded up herself. The Dames settled down for some serious eating.

"Now that we've discussed business, let's gossip."

"It's about frickin' time," Lynn said, looking directly at Susan.

"Susan, the update on Steve please. And when you're done, I have a little news about Dr. Tom." The Dames stopped eating and stared. It seems Susan wasn't the only one thinking of romance.

CHAPTER 18

The Spring Rooster and the Boy Toy

Susan gave a quick update on Steve: their video chats, phone calls, and e-mails—all leading to a meeting when Steve was scheduled to speak at the Home and Garden show in February.

She filled them in on his job, his award, his ex, his beautiful home; she even showed them pictures of him and his dogs, all the unimportant details that she knew they loved to hear.

She kept the important stuff to herself. Before Susan could trust him again they had to talk honestly about why Steve broke off their engagement. When he moved to Chicago, Steve was depressed and angry with himself. He buried his feelings by working and drinking too much. He sold out when he married his socialite wife, forgetting who he was and what his real passions and values were. After his marriage fell apart, Steve went to counseling to understand and subsequently forgive himself. Because Steve had done the "work," this long distance relationship felt safe and familiar. He was proving to be a good friend. And it was so comforting to have a positive and loving history. Many of their conversations went back to the good times they had together before the accident.

Susan shared with him her physical pain after multiple surgeries and her disappointment and anger about never being able to walk again. She was furious with the car's driver, a drunken entitled politician. She explained the financial settlement and how she hid in her apartment to avoid having to deal with stares and questions. Like Steve, she immersed herself in her work. Her beloved technology became family and temporarily filled the void. She told him about the Dames and their special bond without telling him, of course, about their "projects." Steve listened; he cried with her and laughed at the many stories she shared about her recovery. It was exactly what they needed to heal.

However, to actually see Steve in person was a terrifying prospect. What if he was repulsed by her atrophied limbs? What if he looked at her with pity? She couldn't stand that. Susan had too much on her plate right now to worry about the February reunion; she'd tackle that after the "extermination" was completed.

Before Steve's flirtatious e-mails and the downright sexy phone calls, she had no idea that she even had sexual feelings any more. After menopause and the accident, she felt sexually neutered. The doctors told her that she could still have sex given a patient and loving partner, but she hadn't had a partner, let alone a patient and loving one. Maybe she would some day. Until then she was thrilled to be having sexy phone calls and e-mails.

"Are you nuts? Why are you waiting so long? You're no spring chicken and neither is he. Or would he be a spring rooster? My advice: Go for the rooster and soon," Lynn said.

"Lynn, a hen is a female chicken, so chicken works for both genders," Karen said.

"Aren't you just foul!" Lynn said, thoroughly amused at her pathetic pun. The others not so much.

"He's busy with several projects and can't get away any sooner. And ... well ... we're busy planning this."

"You're just scared. I don't blame you. Take your time," Margaret said as she was thinking about Dr. Tom and their upcoming Saturday night dinner date. *Susan has more time to*

119

waste—maybe. Maybe we should all "Seize the day."At my age I don't know how much time I have left.

"Enough about me and Steve," Susan said, looking at Margaret. "Tell us all about the good doctor."

"Well, he is a good doctor. My last x-ray was inconclusive about whether I needed surgery. There was some evidence of healing, but the gap between the broken bones was still significant. If in another month the bones aren't beginning to fuse, I'll have a rod and screws put in. And it's two more weeks at least for the crutches; plus I have to continue wearing the stinky boot."

"Isn't that the name of a play and movie?" Lynn asked. The Dames hooted. "What's so funny?"

"That's *Kinky Boots*."

"I knew that."

"I spray air freshener in the damn thing every morning and that helps a little. So I'm wearing socks most of the time, to cut down on the sweat."

Thank god, Margaret sweats. She is human after all. "Enough with the medical stuff. Has he asked you out on a date?" Lynn asked with her usual sensitivity.

"Well, he has actually, and that's why he referred me to another orthopedic specialist. I didn't know that it was against so many rules to date a patient. When he explained it, it made sense. I met the new doctor and she's great, so now we can see each other with no worries."

"Tell us about him," Susan said.

"Well, he's been divorced for about five years. His ex-wife has remarried. They had two children, both girls, who also became doctors. No grandchildren. He lives in a condo in downtown St. Paul, loves classical music and jazz, hates green peppers, and wants to learn how to play the piano."

"Wow, you've learned a lot in a short amount of time. How old is he?" Karen asked.

"A bit younger than I am; actually quite a bit younger."

"Come on, Margaret, spill it," Susan said.

"He's sixty-two."

"You've got yourself a boy toy!" Karen said, laughing. "What fun!"

"Good for you," Lynn said.

"I think it's time for a toast," Susan said. The Dames refilled their glasses. "To Love... I think the Honeymoon wine is working its magic."

Once the Dames helped Margaret clean up and said their good-byes, Margaret brought her phone to her easy chair and waited for Tom to call after his evening rounds. Margaret looked forward to these nightly chats with great anticipation; she hadn't dated much since her last husband died ten years ago, though she did have occasional liaisons with a former lover. Her impish streak surfaced when she entertained the Dames; she knew they snooped when they used the powder room, so she left out lubricants that indicated she was still sexually active. If they only knew the truth!

Actually Margaret felt like a teenager waiting for the phone to ring. She curtailed social activities to wait for the phone call, and when Tom phoned, they talked for hours, easily discussing almost everything. She told him about her childhood, her college adventures, and eventually her marriages, her sadness about not being able to have children, her fears about getting old and dying.

Tom listened and didn't try to tell her what to do or feel or give advice; he simply listened, a very sexy quality in a man.

And she did the same for him. She learned about his parents, their expectations, his marriage and divorce, his children, his spiritual and political beliefs, favorite foods—all the things people talk about when they're new in a relationship. Margaret had no idea where this was going or if it was going anywhere; she just knew she was enjoying the ride.

Then there was their dinner date Saturday night at the Lexington. She'd give the stinky boot an extra squirt of air freshener. Maybe she'd get to use those lubricants after all.

CHAPTER 19

First Date Confessions

Late Saturday afternoon when Margaret was getting ready for her dinner date, the phone rang. It was Tom.

"Margaret, sorry to call so late, but I just got out of emergency surgery, a car accident, and I'm totally worn out. Any chance we could reschedule?"

"Sure. But here's another option: You could come over here, have a glass of wine, put your feet up, and I could order in. I seem to remember you like comfort food, and it sounds like you could use some comforting. When I was a kid, my favorite comfort food was meatloaf and scalloped potatoes."

"Make that mashed potatoes and we have a deal."

"Deal. What time works for you?"

"How about seven? I'll cancel our reservation at the Lex."

"Perfect. See you in a few hours."

Margaret made the necessary calls: one to the building restaurant to have the dinner delivered at six-thirty and another to Tiff so she could set the table on the balcony since it was such a beautiful evening. Margaret could keep everything warm in the oven. That way the apartment would smell like she actually prepared the meal herself. First impressions and all that. Culinary ambience for sure. Then she went to change into something "more comfortable."

Precisely at 7p.m. Tom buzzed her apartment. She loved a man who was on time.

I have the first date jitters. Settle down, Girl. She answered the door, wearing a pair of expensive capris, a turquoise cotton oversized shirt, and a freshly sprayed stinky boot. With some dangly turquoise and silver earrings and her tousled Meg Ryan style wig, she looked young, fresh, lovely, and only moderately handicapped.

And there he was, a tired but handsome doctor carrying an impressive bottle of California Cabernet.

"Come on in. You must be exhausted." She gave him a big hug. He smelled clean with a scent of something she couldn't quite place, something woodsy and citrusy like if you were camping in the woods and eating grapefruit for breakfast, lunch and dinner.

Tom walked in, looked briefly at the art work and expensive furniture and then walked directly to the wall of glass. "Wow, this is beautiful. What a view of the river!" My condo has a nice view of Mears Park, but nothing as spectacular as this. Stunning," Tom said, but he was actually looking at Margaret, not the view, when he said that.

"Let's open your wine and take it to the balcony. This is a perfect time of night to enjoy the view. We could actually eat out here, if you'd like."

"I like."

"We're up high enough that we avoid mosquitos." Margaret went into the kitchen, opened the wine, poured them each a glass.

Tom followed her and peeked at the meal warming in the oven. "It smells delicious."

"First date confession: I can't cook, but I can make a nice salad, and I do throw together a mean cheese plate. You'll have to help me carry all this stuff."

"No problem. First date confession: I can cook." Margaret smiled. *On time and a cook who happens to smell wonderful. This might just work.*

She handed him both glasses of wine and gimped out to the balcony, settling into her comfortable lounger. Tom returned to the kitchen for the bottle and the cheese plate.

"How did you manage to set such a beautiful table?" He nodded to the table with the yellow linen table cloth, the flower centerpiece, and candles.

"I have a little help by the name of Tiff. I called her right after your phone call and she ran down to set the table. She's been a life-saver. Tell me about the emergency surgery."

"I got called in around three. Seems this kid was in a terrible car accident and broke his femur. In the old days doctors used traction, but now we insert a steel rod. He had a relatively simple break, but the surgery still lasted two hours. Poor kid. He'll have a long recovery with lots of physical therapy, but he's young. That always helps," He sat in the cushioned lounger, sipped his wine, ate some cheese and crackers and breathed deeply. "It feels really good to relax."

"Time for a toast: To healing femurs and to the doctors who make it possible."

They conversed comfortably for nearly an hour. They talked, laughed, and sat in companionable silence, watching the sun get steadily lower over the river, the colors increasing in intensity with each minute.

"Getting hungry?"

"Starving."

"I'd better check on the food, but I'm going to need your help again. Let's dish up in the kitchen so you don't have to carry so much."

"Better idea. Why don't you sit here and enjoy the sunset, and I'll dish up the food."

"What a great idea! First date confession number two: I love being waited on when I'm wounded. The salad is in the fridge."

"Don't worry. I'll find what I need."

They had just finished dinner when someone rang Margaret's doorbell.

"I can't imagine who that might be."

"Do you want me to get it?"

"No, just stay out here and relax. It's a beautiful night."

She went to the door and found a disheveled and upset Tiff, her mascara running down her face and a handprint clearly visible on her cheek.

"What in the world happened to you?" Margaret said. "You'd better come in." Margaret lead her into the kitchen.

"Is your doctor friend still here? I don't want to bother you."

"He's relaxing on the balcony. Sit down. What happened?"

"Short version: Bob and I got in a fight. He wanted me to 'meet' a few of his friends tonight and I didn't feel like it. He got mad, I got mad, words were said and he slapped me. He's never done that before," Tiff said, and she broke into tears again.

"How about a cup of tea or a glass of wine? We can talk for a bit."

"Tea sounds good. Won't your guest mind?"

"He'll be fine."

Margaret put the kettle on while Tiff told her about the argument.

"I don't think you should go back there tonight. Do you want to stay here?"

Tiff looked at her and said, "Would you mind? I don't know if he's still in the apartment and quite frankly he kinda scared me. I don't want to confront him again tonight. We both need some time to cool off."

"Is it necessary to tell him where you are?"

"I'll just phone him on his land line and say I'm okay. He's probably gone out with his friends.

Don't worry I won't tell him where I am. I don't want him pounding on your door, especially if he's been drinking."

"What a mess. Why don't you use the bathroom and wash your face? I'll get you a toothbrush and some towels."

"Thanks, Margaret, for everything. I must look awful."

"You're a beautiful woman inside and out. You deserve to be treated with respect. Don't you ever forget that."

When Tiff left to use the bathroom, Margaret went out to check on Tom, but he was sound asleep.

After Tiff returned, she quietly cleared the balcony table while Tom snored away. She loaded the dishwasher and cleaned up the leftovers, helping herself to the meatloaf and salad. When she finished her snack, she excused herself and went to the guest bedroom to settle in for the night.

Margaret went out to the balcony and gently tapped Tom's shoulder. He woke up, rubbed his eyes, and looked at her with affection.

"Sorry, I told you I was tired. I'm embarrassed that I actually fell asleep on our first date."

"I loved our first date," she said, sitting in the chair next to him. "Let's just enjoy the sunset for awhile."

"First date confession #2: I snore," Tom said, taking Margaret's hand.

"I know."

"First date confession #3: I have a stinky boot."

"I know," Tom said, laughing. Margaret leaned over and playfully punched his arm.

CHAPTER 20

Crossing Lines

Tiff and Margaret were having their morning coffee when the phone rang. Tiff looked nervous. "What if it's Bob? I didn't tell him where I was, but he could have figured it out."

"I'll answer it," Margaret said, ready to take him on if necessary. She had already planned to take him out.

"Tell me about your date. Was it wonderful? Did he kiss you goodnight? Was there chemistry? Will you go out again?" Lynn took a breath and a drink of tea.

"Whoa, slow down, Lynn. One question at a time." Tiff looked at Margaret and grinned, relieved it wasn't Bob.

"Well, it's a long story, but I'll give you the short version. We canceled the reservation at the Lex because he was too tired from his stressful day, including an emergency surgery at three. He came over here for dinner instead."

"'I'm too tired,'" Lynn said in a whiny voice, imitating her philandering ex. "Too tired, my ass; he was boffing his bimbo babe. It must be a doctor thing."

"Don't make this about your ex. Tom isn't like that."

"You're right. Can I get a do-over?"

"If you must."

"I must." Lynn sighed loudly. "An intimate dinner for two, how romantic. Did you cook? What did you make? Did you have sex?" Lynn fired off the questions with machine gun velocity. The sex question was the one she wanted to ask

127

first, but decided she needed to ease into it, which meant she said whatever popped into her brain; she was filter free and proud.

"No, ordered meatloaf from our restaurant, and no. Now are you happy?"

"I won't be happy until you have sex," Lynn said, laughing. "When's our next planning session?"

ADD alert.I don't want to continue this conversation.

"Sooner rather than later. Would you please call Susan and Karen for me and tell them it's Happy Hour here at five. I'll explain then." Margaret hung up before Lynn could fire off more questions.

"Now what are we going to do about you and Bob?" Margaret said to Tiff, who was tidying the already tidy kitchen.

"I have some big decisions to make, not just about Bob, but about my life. I don't want to go back to doing hair and I don't want to be an 'escort' any more."

"About that, Tiff... "

Tiff interrupted Margaret before she could finish her sentence. "People get the wrong idea about being an 'escort.' The old coots paid me to be their 'eye candy' nothing else. Occasionally, I'd give them a hug or a kiss on the cheek, but there was no sex."

Then why were there birth control pills in the bathroom? Something is definitely wrong here. I think she's embarrassed and ashamed. She's lying to protect herself and Bob. Could she be having sex with Bob? That's too disgusting to even think about.

"Most of the time they just wanted to show me off and to talk. It was easy work and it paid well, though it was expensive to keep up appearances. Sometimes I even enjoyed getting to know them, but I want control over my own life. I don't want Bob or someone else telling me who to see and what to do. I want and need my own place. It's time. That was really obvious after last night."

"Could you go back to the salon until you save enough to get your own place? Or could you get a roommate to share rent?"

"The salon where I used to work said I could come back whenever I wanted. I suppose I could work there the days I don't work for you. I might be able to stand it if I worked part-time. And I could ask around if there's anybody who wants a roommate."

"Makes sense for the time being, at least. Once I find out if I need surgery, which should be in the next few weeks, we can make a more definite plan. If I have surgery, I'll need to increase your hours because I won't be able to put any weight on this foot for six weeks. So let's keep our Tuesday, Thursday, Friday schedule for right now. As for your going back to Bob's, let's see how today goes. You need to have a heart to heart with him and set some boundaries. I don't want him using or abusing you. He crossed a line yesterday and you need to call him on it. Remember you can always call me, day or night."

"I think I'll head on upstairs and see how it goes. He's always been very sweet to me; he and Edith saved me, you know, and they paid for cosmetology school. I owe them a lot; if Edith were alive, this never would have happened. He hasn't been the same since she passed."

She definitely thinks of him as her savior. She is protecting him. Stockholm Syndrome?

"Good luck, Tiff. Remember I'm here if you need me."

"Thanks for everything, Margaret." Tiff gave Margaret a hug and left to confront the man she perceived as her benefactor who in reality was her abuser.

* * *

"So what's the rush, Margaret? You made it sound rather urgent on the phone," Lynn said as she carried in her favorite frozen cheesecake. "It's just Sara Lee. I didn't have time to go to a bakery."

129

"And you're late because... " Karen asked.

"Looks like someone is having a bad day," Lynn scowled at Karen. "For your information, my daughter called to complain about her husband just as I was leaving. I am so glad mine is dead. I mean that in the best possible way."

The Dames were seated and having a glass of white wine. Margaret had already answered all their questions about Tom; Susan had checked in as well, so everyone was up to date on their pals' budding romances, leaving Karen and Lynn noticeably jealous and somewhat cranky.

"Help yourself to wine, Lynn. I wanted to wait until everybody arrived before explaining the need for this spur of the moment planning session. You see, last night Tiff interrupted my date."

"So that explains why you didn't have sex," Lynn said. Karen and Susan hooted at Lynn.

"I don't know why that's so funny. You both were thinking it," Lynn said.

"You. You're what's so funny," Karen said. "Now I want to hear about Tiff, so be quiet."

"As I was saying, Tiff came to me upset and hurt. She and Bob had fought and Bob slapped her." Margaret went on to summarize Tiff's problems and to explain Tiff spent the night without Bob's knowledge.

"Tiff called me this afternoon, and she said Bob had apologized for his behavior. She said she felt safe for the moment. I've assured her that she can stay with me again if she needs to."

"Now I get it. We need to get this show on the road before things escalate," Susan said. "I think we're ready. We've got a plan and I've got the placebos that look like real aspirin."

Susan took the bottle of placebos from her purse and showed everyone. "I have plenty if anyone wants to try one. They don't taste like sugar at all." Lynn held out her hand for a sample.

"You're right," Lynn said. "He'll never know the difference."

"I say we try for Operation Switcheroo this Thursday."

"To Operation Switcheroo." The Dames clinked glasses.

"To Mr. Miller, aka His Assholiness." The Dames clinked again.

"To Tiff's health." The Dames clinked a third time.

"Enough with the toasts," Margaret said, once again insisting on order.

"Party pooper," Lynn mumbled.

"I heard that. Sorry to rain on your parade, Lynn, but we need to meet on Wednesday to review the plan and finalize everything. And Susan, bring Miss Dottie; she's part of this as well," Margaret said.

"Now that Margaret has brought us back to reality again, we can proceed to the cheesecake. I'll slice and serve," Lynn said, grumbling and tooting as she went into the kitchen.

"To another great exit fart," Karen said as she took another swig of wine. The Dames hooted.

"I heard that," Lynn said from the kitchen.

CHAPTER 21

Operation Switcheroo

Wednesday
1900 hours

"Let's go over the plan one more time. Karen, would you do the honors?" Karen went to the storage area where Margaret kept the whiteboard, and the Dames began making their last minute list:

> *1. S phones M @11:30. T walks D.*

"Can't you just write their names? All these initials hurt my brain and give me a headache," Lynn whined.

"Everything hurts your brain," Karen responded. "Is this better?"

> *2. Marg switches purses while Tiff walks Dot.*
> *Marg calls Mill's apt. If home, abort mission.*

"Better, but still too many Ms," Lynn said. "Use Bob for Mr. Miller."

"Okay, okay," Karen said, making the corrections. "Happy now?"

"Where will Tiff's purse and keys be?" Lynn asked.

"I'll put her purse in the bathroom linen closet. When you're done, put the key back. Oh dear, I just thought of something. How will I switch the purses back? Any ideas?"

"We'll need another distraction. We can't use Susan again so it will have to be one of us."

"I could pretend to have computer problems and ask her to come to my apartment to help me. Kids her age know all about computers. What if I want to open a Facebook account? Would that work?"

"I think it might," Karen said. "Do you really want to open a Facebook account?"

"No, but I'll take one for the team." Lynn and Karen slapped hands.

"Okay. You have time to think of a good reason to ask for Tiff's help. Just make sure she's gone long enough so that I can make the switch."

3. *Marg &Tiff, run errands for one hr.*

"How will we know when you leave?" Lynn asked. "And when you get back."

"I'll call you and let it ring once," Margaret said.

"You'll have to tell us what purse she's using. Just say the color."

4. *Lynn & Kar get Bob's keys, search Bob's apt.*
Count pills & switch.

"How are we going to get into your apartment?" Karen asked.

"I have an extra set that I'll give you right now," Margaret limped into the kitchen and returned with the extra set. "Let's try the apartment key out, just in case." It worked.

"I remember right after I moved in I got a couple of extra keys made and they didn't work. Good idea to test it," Susan said.

"Right. Now don't lose the damn key, Lynn."

"Why is everything always my fault?"

"Need I remind you who forgot her cell phone when we went mushroom hunting? And who loses her car keys every day?"

"Okay, okay, point taken. Karen, since you're so damn responsible, you keep the key." Lynn handed the key to Karen and she put it in her pants pocket.

5. *Sue goes to lobby after Marg &Tiff return as a precaution in case Bob comes home early.*

* * *

Thursday
0900 hours

"Like the outfit, Lynn," Karen said. They had decided to meet up in Karen's kitchen at nine for coffee and moral support.

"I've been researching military slang for this project and thought I might buy some cammies."

"Why would you want to wear jammies?"

"Not jammies, cammies. Your hearing is getting worse. You know camouflage clothes, but I wouldn't wear them again, so I thought I'd go for the cat burglar look. Do you think it's too much?"

Lynn was wearing all black, including a long-sleeved turtleneck and black knit gloves. The outside temp was eighty-five degrees with a very high dew point.

"It's eighty-five degrees today with a heat index of almost 100. What if someone sees us? Don't you think they'll think your outfit's weird? We don't want to call attention to ourselves at all. So, yes, I do think it's too much.

"Something more appropriate like *moi*." Pretending she was a model, Karen twirled in her white capris, tank top, and a short sleeved hot pink hand knit sweater that barely covered her flabby upper arms. Lynn rolled her eyes.

"Okay. I'll go home and change into something less conspicuous. Should I bring a moonbeam? That's military talk for a flashlight."

"It's daytime, Lynn."

"Sounds to me like you need a little more rack time. Maybe that would improve your mood. See you in about ten minutes."

"Bring a bag for carrying the placebos and the aspirin."

"Copy that."

Karen's flat was unlike the others because it was much smaller and furnished by a garage sale junkie. No professional decorators for her. It was beyond eclectic and well into funky. Her kitchen was painted a bright yellow, her walls decorated with variety of old metal and wooden signs. Her favorite was a blue dance hall sign from the 1930s that said, "Intoxicants Prohibited." The Dames really got a charge out of that, considering they loved their intoxicants. The Dames also got a charge out of the sign above Karen's bedroom door that said, "No Trespassing."

In addition to her sign obsession, Karen collected chicken memorabilia. Chickens nested on her shelves, on her counters, on her dishes, glassware, and on the walls. She had a ceramic chicken head named Henrietta, her "guardian chicken," mounted on her wall. Karen had a rooster clock that crowed on the hour. Her aprons and dish towels had chickens on them. Karen was to chickens as Lynn was to cats. That's why most of the Happy Hours were held in either Margaret's or Susan's apartments. It was to avoid the chickens and, of course, the smell of cat pee in Lynn's flat.

The rest of Karen's one bedroom apartment was filled with weird folk art and a mixture of original painted furniture from the mid-1800s and upholstered furniture from previous abodes.

Ten minutes later Lynn arrived wearing baggy Bermuda shorts and an over-sized t-shirt the Dames gave her that said: "What don't you understand about ADD. Oh, look, there's a chicken."

"Considering your obsession with all things clucky, I thought this was appropriate. An improvement?" Lynn said, imitating Karen's previous twirl.

"Just barely. Want to watch some HGTV while we wait for Margaret's phone call? It will help us relax."

In the next two and a half hours, Karen had three phone calls: one from her bored married daughter, one from a telemarketer, and one from her pharmacy telling her that her prescription was ready. Each time the Dames jumped in anticipation.

* * *

Thursday
1155 hours

The phone rang once. Karen picked up and Margaret said, "Denim."

"Hooah!" Lynn said, jumping up.

"Karen, cell phone."

"Check."

"Placebos."

"Check."

"Margaret's key."

Karen hurried to her purse and rummaged through it. "The key's gotta be here somewhere. I put it in my purse when we were at Margaret's so I wouldn't lose it." She took everything out of her purse and put it on the yellow Formica kitchen table, a relic from her parents' house. No key.

"And I'm the one who can't be responsible? You should have the key ready to go. This is a Charlie fox trot."

"What the hell does that mean?"

"A clean way of saying a cluster fuck."

"Point taken. Dammit, how could I be so stupid?"

"Don't panic. Let's think. What were you wearing last night? Could you have put it in your pocket?"

"That must be what happened. I'll go check." Karen left to search her bedroom. "Shit, I put those pants in the wash." She ran to the washing machine in the utility room and came out grinning and slightly damp, but she was holding the key. "Now we're in business! Let's get going. Have I told you lately that you're brilliant?"

136

Both women were puffing by the time they got to Margaret's apartment. They went directly to the bathroom linen closet and found a very heavy set of keys in Tiff's denim purse.

"Now how do we know which one's the key to Miller's apartment?"

"Well, we've got Margaret's key to compare it to. It should look somewhat similar. What do you think? Could this be it? Look, this one has a red dot of nail polish on it. I'll bet money that's the one. She is a cosmetologist after all. Let's go."

"Hooah!"

* * *

Thursday
1215 hours

The Dames used the steps rather than the elevator to avoid seeing any of their neighbors. In a senior high rise, most tenants took the easy way: the elevator.

By the time they got to the ninth floor, they were gasping for breath once again.

"I have to start using the exercise room. When we're done with Mr. Miller, I think you and I should meet to exercise every other day at least. Think of it as a kind of boot camp for the elderly. Check your schedule when we get home," Lynn said.

"This is not the time to discuss exercise plans," Karen said as they approached Mr. Miller's flat. She fumbled the keys, dropping them onto the hallway carpet.

"Here, let me. You're too nervous." Lynn took the key with the red dot, inserted it into the lock, and slowly opened the door. "You were right. Good call." She slowly opened the door and walked into the darkened apartment. She finally found a light switch. "Anyone here?" she yelled.

"No one but us chickens," Karen yelled back. Lynn jumped. "Now who's a nervous Nelly?"

"Very funny," Lynn said. "Would you look at this place? Margaret wasn't kidding about the flowers; they're everywhere."

"We can't spend time criticizing the decorating. We need to make the switch and get outta here."

"Okay, where do we start?"

"Most people keep their aspirin in their kitchens, bathrooms, and bedrooms," Karen said. "I'll take the kitchen. You take the master bedroom and bath and I'll take Tiff's bedroom and bath. Try not to disturb anything too much. On the double." Karen was getting the hang of military slang. The Dames went off on their separate missions.

"Eww, Bob has pornography in the drawer of his night stand. I can't believe people can even do that!" Lynn said, looking at the pictures.

"Focus, Lynn."

Karen searched the kitchen cupboards on both sides of the sink and found a bottle of aspirin half filled. She quickly dumped the aspirin into the bag and substituted the placebos. *Easy peasy. Now on to Tiff's bedroom.*

Tiff's bedroom was well-organized with all her clothes hung up neatly. The bed was made, pillows fluffed, knickknacks dusted. She searched the night stand and found nothing of interest except a vibrator.

Karen remembered her second husband, what's his name, didn't have a clue about her vibrator. When he'd be watching football she'd be upstairs squealing in delight while he would be cursing the static on the TV. He never figured out that the her vibrator was the source of the interference. She tried it on her bum shoulder. *Feels good. Focus, Karen, focus.*

"How you doing, Lynn?"

"Found two bottles in the master bath and made the switch."

Now on to Tiff's bathroom. Karen was going through the medicine cabinet when she heard the door open and the sounds of a radio playing loud rap music. *Oh shit!*

Karen had to think fast. She knew they would be discovered, so she had to come up with some kind of cover. Who would be in the apartment snooping around? *Overnight guests? Exterminators? That's exactly what we are. Too close to the truth, but we could be newly hired decorators, that's who. Now if Lynn will just go along with me.* Karen walked into the master and whispered, "Follow my lead. We're decorators."

"Copy that. I've always want to be a decorator. It's a good thing we watched HGTV right before we left."

"Lynn, I think we've seen enough to get an idea of what Bob wants," Karen said loudly.

The radio stopped and a woman yelled, "Who's there?"

Karen and Lynn walked into the living room. "His decorators and who might you be, young lady?"

"I'm his cleaning lady."

"Bob asked us to walk through his apartment and give him an estimate on some re-decorating. The poor man lost his beloved wife a few years ago and finally decided he needed to move on to something more masculine. Do you know Bob personally?"

"No, I've only talked to him once on the phone. I come every Thursday when he's gone. He leaves me a list and a check. I've never met him."

"I'm curious how long cleaning his apartment takes; my cleaning lady insists I vacate the apartment for four hours. That seems a bit excessive to me,"

"That's pretty standard for an apartment or home this size. I ask Bob to stay away that long as well, so I don't think your cleaning lady is ripping you off." Then she took a careful look at Lynn's t-shirt and at Lynn. "You don't look like a decorator."

"Sorry about that. I was in the midst of cleaning my apartment when Karen gave me the call about Bob. I hurried here, not bothering to change." Lynn pointed to the living room and said, "We'll remove this dated wallpaper, paint the living room a light gray-blue, get rid of these heavy drapes, pull up this disgusting carpet, add some wood floors, I think some crown molding, leather furniture with some accent pillows to bring in some color. What do you think about the popcorn ceilings, Karen?"

"Get rid of them. We'll need to add some overhead lighting, and the kitchen is a total mess. We've got our notes and are ready to come up with a plan and an estimate." Karen looked at the cleaning lady, "I don't how you do it with all the clutter that's around here. You have my utmost respect."

"There are a lot of flowers ... too many for me and I love flowers. Too much stuff for my taste."

"What's your name?" Karen asked.

"Maria."

"Nice to meet you, Maria." Karen held out her hand.

"Likewise," Lynn said, doing the same. "And for the master bedroom and bath...," Lynn continued to spout decorator-talk as they exited Bob's apartment.

* * *

Thursday
1300 hours

They quickly got on the elevator and went directly to Margaret's apartment, deposited Tiff's keys in her purse, and went back to Karen's, all in silence, an unusual occurrence for the Dames.

"Talk about a soup sandwich!" Lynn said as soon as they opened the door. Once inside they both burst into hysterical laughter. "We made it in time. I wasn't sure we would, especially after you couldn't find the key and then we had to climb all those steps. And the small talk with Maria? I still can't believe we ran right into the cleaning lady."

"I hope we pulled it off. She could describe us to Bob and we'd be toast, but I think we convinced her. All that decorator jargon. How much HGTV do you watch anyway?"

"A lot. *Fixer Upper*'s my favorite along with *Rehab Addict* and the *Property Brothers*. Those guys are hot!"

"The important thing is we got the majority, if not all, of the aspirin, in spite of the cleaning lady. All I saw in Tiff's bath were Midol, some vitamins, and her birth control pills. Talk about a close call. My heart is still pounding." Karen paused a bit. "I just thought of something. Are you sure you put the keys in the right purse?"

"It was the orange one, right?"

Karen blanched.

"Sit down; you look pale. I was just joshin' ya. I put the keys in the blue denim."

"You can be downright cruel sometimes. I almost fainted." Karen's color was slowly returning.

"All that's left of Operation Switcheroo is a phone call from Margaret telling us they're back. Then you call her back, asking for computer help from Tiff; Margaret switches purses and we're good to go! Hooah!"

"What does that mean anyway?"

"Not a clue. It's just fun to say."

CHAPTER 22

To Surprise or Not to Surprise

Three weeks later

One week after surgery Margaret was resting with her foot on the leather ottoman, feeling a bit low. Diagnosis: a severe case of Cabin Fever, something even Dr. Tom couldn't fix. Unable to put any weight on the bum foot and ankle, she was destined to use crutches in the house and a ridiculous scooter when she went out in public. Unable to accept her aging, she wasn't about to accept something akin to a walker. She was so incapacitated she couldn't even do her usual workout with her personal trainer.

Her neighbors had been more than generous with their casseroles, cookies, flowers, cards, and good wishes, but she was sick of being dependent. She was sick of being sick. Plus, there was this air of uncertainty and unease while the Dames were waiting for something to happen to Mr. Miller. Passive extermination was highly over-rated. Too bad they couldn't think of a way to speed things up.

Tiff was vacuuming and Margaret was bored, bored, bored. She'd had two more "dates" with Tom, if you counted ordering pizza and Thai take-out "dates." He was always considerate, punctual, cheerful, basically a nice guy. Tom was a guy you could depend on to help you out. Margaret filed that away because she knew there would come a day when she would need just that kind of guy.

Back in Chicago Steve was packing his suitcase to drive to Minneapolis for a business trip. In addition to his business apparel, he was packing some casual clothes because he was intending to surprise his former fiancé, maybe take her to a few familiar haunts, like the bar where they met. Or would she have to take him in her modified van? He wasn't exactly sure what her disability would mean to their relationship. Simple things like transportation and general mobility were question marks to say nothing of complicated things like sex. Just how self-sufficient was she? How was she coping physically and emotionally? His mind raced with questions and the excitement of seeing the woman he once loved. He remembered how comfortable he felt in her presence, how he trusted and admired her, how she was his best friend. He realized he still felt that comfort and admiration. Their daily e-mails and nightly video chats were the highlights of his day. She looked beautiful, just as he remembered her.

Pre-accident Susan loved surprises and spontaneity. When they were first dating, he left for a week long convention in New York. The speakers were so terrible, the information so repetitive, he decided to take an early flight home to surprise her. At the time she was living in a town home near Lake Minnetonka. When he showed up unannounced, she squealed with delight, jumped into his arms and whisked him off to the bedroom. Later, they opened a bottle of bubbly and barbecued steaks in her courtyard. That night sealed the deal for Steve; he knew that his next surprise would be an engagement ring.

That surprise came in front of a camp fire just outside Bayfield, Wisconsin. September along the shores of Lake Superior was breathtakingly beautiful, the fall color at its peak. It was post bug, pre snow perfect. After a delightful morning of hiking and having lunch at Maggie's, their favorite Bayfield restaurant, they settled on an afternoon "nap" in the camper and a dinner of smoked fish, cheese, bread, fruit and wine on the picnic table provided by the sparsely populated campsite. While sipping the last of their wine in front of the fire, Steve dropped to his knees and proposed. Susan, thoroughly charmed by the gesture and the two carat diamond solitaire, accepted his proposal.

That was then. Now was a little more complicated. They had both changed and he was terrified that he might scare her off. She had a right to be skittish about him and his cowardly retreat just when she needed him most. He still didn't fully understand his decision to leave. He didn't want to believe he was the kind of guy who hit the road when the road got bumpy. But he did. Then there was his divorce. Did he do it again with Mary? They were such different people with different interests, values, and beliefs. He didn't want to believe he was That Guy.

His therapist talked about facing his fears. Steve just wasn't exactly sure what he was afraid of. Commitment? Inadequacy? Failure? Maybe surprising Susan wasn't such a good idea after all. He could go to his business meetings and Susan would be none the wiser. Then they could go back to being techno-buddies. Steve had this internal conversation again and again all the way to Minneapolis.

As soon as he got near Mendota Heights late in the afternoon, he checked into his hotel, got settled, and drove to Susan's condo. He sat in the parking area and once again went over his options: to surprise or not. *What the hell, no guts, not glory,* he thought as he punched in Susan's cell phone number. He would ask her out for dinner; they both had to eat after all.

"Margaret, this is an emergency. Steve just called me and he's in the parking lot ... our parking lot. This isn't supposed to happen; he should be in Chicago not here. I told him I had an engagement and I'd call him back. Meanwhile he's waiting in his car in our parking lot. What do I do?"

"Take a deep breath and try to relax. First of all, this isn't an emergency. It's an incredible opportunity. It's a chance for you to discover if Steve is the man for you. You don't have to wait until February to find out. Second, you are a beautiful, successful, attractive woman who can do whatever she wants. You have choices."

"What would you do?"

"I'd go for it. But you and I are different people. Personally, I think you'd be nuts to let this opportunity slip through your fingers."

Susan paused for a minute, pondering Margaret's advice. Then she blurted, "What should I wear? What do I feed him? I don't have any food in the house, just junk."

"Good choice—to go for it. Wear one of your pretty new blouses and order up from our restaurant. Open a bottle of wine. You'll be fine, but I want to hear all about it after he leaves... if he leaves."

"Okay. Okay. I can do this," Susan said mainly to herself. "I feel like I did right before going to Prom with David Danielson."

"I understand. That's the way I felt before my first date with Tom. Slightly nauseous, right?"

"It's weird how we're still young on the inside."

"You don't have time for philosophizing. Get changed, girl, and invite the boy up!"

CHAPTER 23

"You're probably right."

The doorbell rang. Dottie barked. Susan opened the door and saw Steve holding a bouquet of slightly wilted flowers. Dottie sniffed as dogs do and declared Steve a good guy by wagging her tail enthusiastically.

"Hey, girl. You must be Dottie," he said, scratching behind her ears. "Pretty dog." Then he looked at Susan and said, "Pretty woman." Susan looked away unsure what to say or do.

"Do you shake, girl?"

Susan laughed and put out her hand.

When Dottie heard the word 'shake,' she sat obediently and put out her paw. "Good girl, or should I say good girls." Steve grinned at Susan. As soon as he praised Dottie, she rolled on her back for a tummy rub.

"Just so you know, I don't do tummy rubs," Susan laughed, trying to ease the awkwardness she felt.

Then he looked at Susan with tears in his eyes and said, "Sorry about the wilted flowers, but they'll perk up when they're put in water. You just have to make a new cut and maybe add some plant food. I think there's some in the flower wrapper," he said, rattling the cellophane. "Am I babbling?" Steve said as he pulled on his ear. Susan smiled, remembering that endearing nervous gesture.

"A little, but I understand."

"May I come in?"

"Of course. I must have misplaced my manners."

Steve walked into the foyer and surveyed the apartment first from a distance and then more closely. He walked into her living/media room, looking at the art, the furnishings, the computers. "This is absolutely beautiful. Much better than the magazine photographs. Who designed the interior?"

"I did mostly, but I had help from an architect who specializes in wheelchair accessible designs. My bathroom is amazing. Would you like to see it?" Steve watched with pride as she wheeled into her beautiful bedroom and en suite with Dottie by her side. Yes, her bathroom and entire apartment were amazing, but they were nothing compared to this beautiful, courageous, talented woman. Now if he could only convince her that he was a changed man.

After the tour, Susan went into the kitchen and took a bottle of her favorite red wine blend and handed it to Steve along with a high tech wine bottle opener. She found a hand blown glass vase and started to arrange the somewhat bedraggled bouquet.

"How do you work this darned thing? I'm used to an old-fashioned cork screw."

"It's easy," Susan said and with an effortless twist opened the bottle. She wheeled to her cupboard and took out two very pretty etched wine glasses and poured them each a glass.

"Since you mentioned something about dinner on the phone, I have to apologize. The cupboard is bare; I was planning to shop tomorrow. We'll have to order from the restaurant downstairs or go out."

"I doubt that your 'cupboard is bare.' It never was. Remember how we used to cook from what we had on hand? We called it garbage food. Let's see what you have in the fridge and pantry."

"I hope there's no sauerkraut in there. Remember the sauerkraut omelet?"

"I'd forgotten about that hideous concoction." They both laughed.

"The challenge is on, as long as you promise no kraut," Susan said, wheeling to the pantry. She pulled out a box of penne pasta, a small jar of mushrooms, and a package of sun dried tomatoes.

In the fridge Steve found a half bag of spinach, an onion, a moldy chunk of cheddar cheese, some sour cream, a quart of milk, three eggs and a few olives.

"Any canned fruit in the pantry?"

"Some peaches."

"Perfect."

"Garbage pasta and garbage pudding. You're on," Susan said as she collected ingredients for the dessert: sugar, vanilla, cornstarch, salt. I'll do dessert and you can do the pasta. Let me do the pudding first since we'll both be needing the stove." Susan whisked the sugar, cornstarch, salt, adding the milk and stirring. When the mixture had thickened and come to a slow boil, she added about a half a cup of the cooked mixture to the whisked egg yolks. Then she added that mixture to the saucepan and boiled for one minute. A few splashes of vanilla and *voila*: pudding! She poured the pudding into parfait glasses, interspersing the drained peaches with the pudding.

"Now, I'll sit back, sip my wine, and enjoy the show!" Susan said as she watched Steve make the sauce. He first poured very hot water over the sun dried tomatoes, making them plump and delicious. Then he sauteed the onions, mushrooms, sliced olives, spinach and tomatoes in olive oil. A few tablespoons of sour cream, the cleaned-up cheddar cheese combined with a little milk made a creamy sauce. He added some dried basil and parsley that he found while Susan was making pudding. Once the pasta was boiled, he added the sauce to create a garbage pasta masterpiece.

Seated at the kitchen table, Steve refreshed their wine and made a toast: "To a long and beautiful life—hopefully together."

Susan smiled and made a toast of her own: "To second chances and more garbage meals."

After helping with the clean-up, Steve yawned discreetly. Dottie was sound asleep under the kitchen table.

"Would you like me to take Dottie out for a quick walk before I leave?"

"That would be great. Thanks."

As soon as Steve left, Susan phoned Margaret and gave her a quick summary of what had happened thus far.

"As soon as he's out the door I want you to come down and we'll debrief. I'll gather the Dames. They're very excited to hear details."

"Will do. See you in a few minutes." Susan smiled. She hadn't been this happy for years.

Steve returned about ten minutes later with a very happy and relieved Dottie.

"Poop and pee report. Successful on both counts." I put the bag in the receptacle across from the lobby. I hope that's okay."

"That's what it's there for. We have quite of few dogs in this community." Susan paused a bit, unsure of what to say next. "Thanks, Steve—for everything."

"This has been wonderful. I'm more tired than I thought after the long drive, so I think I'll say my goodbyes. Thank you so much for the gourmet garbage and the delicious wine. It's nice to know we haven't lost our touch." At that he went to Susan and bent down to kiss her gently on the lips. "How about we try this again tomorrow night? This time I'll take you out."

"Thanks, again, Steve—for everything. Until tomorrow then," Susan pulled him down for another kiss, this one not so gentle.

"Good night, Miss Dottie." Dottie, slut that she was, rolled over to have her tummy rubbed one more time. A quick rub and Steve was out the door.

Susan gave him about fifteen minutes before she headed to Margaret's apartment for a night cap and a Dames' debriefing. Just as she entered Margaret's apartment she saw flashing lights reflected in the floor to ceiling windows and heard the screaming sirens. She saw the Dames on the balcony watching the action.

Her first thought was that something had happened to Steve, but when she joined them on the balcony, she saw EMTs carrying someone out on a stretcher, his face covered with an oxygen mask. She breathed a sigh of relief. *It wasn't Steve.*

"Who is it?" The Dames all started talking at once. Then Margaret pointed to Tiffany running to her car.

The Dames watched as the ambulance drove away. Suddenly, it was quiet as the Dames began to process what they'd done.

"Let's adjourn to the living room, ladies," Margaret said. "We don't want to add to the disturbance."

Once inside they exploded, all talking at once:

"I don't care much about Mr. Miller, but I do feel kind of sorry for Tiffany."

"She really does care for him."

"Collateral damage."

"Don't forget how he treated her."

"She'll be much better off without him."

"You're probably right."

"Now she can get on with her life."

"Maybe we're getting ahead of ourselves."

"You're probably right."

"He might not be dead."

"We shouldn't count our chickens before they hatch."

"You and your damn chickens."

"I say it's time for G&Ts."

"You're probably right."

CHAPTER 24

The BIG ONE

Six months later

For Minnesotans the weather is often the main source of conversation, especially in a political off season, so it was no surprise when severe weather warnings showed up on their TV screens.

"Blizzard warnings for Ramsey and Hennepin counties. Heavy snow and high winds likely." The weather message scrolled on the bottom of Margaret's fifty inch TV screen, disrupting one of their favorite shows: *The Good Wife*.

"I hate when they scroll that shit across the bottom of the screen. It's so annoying," Lynn said as she ate another handful of popcorn.

"How can you eat popcorn after that dinner?"

"I can always eat popcorn. Remember I'm grieving the loss of Lizzy, my sweet kitty." Then in a whisper, "Besides that bean dish was ... "

Just then Margaret walked in the living room. "...that bean dish was... "

"Delicious."

"Why don't I believe you? I thought it was bland and boring. Tom would have known what to do to make it better. I just don't have a feel for cooking."

"That's because you don't have a feel for eating," Lynn

said, noticing for the first time that Margaret seemed to be losing weight.

Ever since Tom was teaching her to how to cook, the Dames had endured *boef bourguignon,* French onion soup and this night's specialty, *cassoulet.* Lynn and Karen didn't see what was so special about beans and chicken or beef stew for that matter, but they were willing to humor Margaret and praised her cooking with enthusiasm. At least Margaret made tasty salads and served superb wines.

"I wish I had that problem. 'Bland,' 'boring,' whatever, I'll eat it. I'm an emotional eater and I still feel awful about having to put Lizzy down."

"Is that the cat who peed all over?"

"No that was Missy. Lizzy was the barfer. I remember one time when I had you girls up for dessert and she hacked up a hairball. I thought you were going to lose your cheesecake." Lynn looked directly at Margaret and laughed.

"So I have a delicate tummy. I admit it."

The show and the conversation were interrupted by a Weather Bulletin, a far more serious interruption than the previous notification:

"The blizzard warning is for real folks," said the station's meteorologist. "This could be the BIG ONE."

"They always say that," Lynn said. "They're probably wrong like they were around Christmas. People were canceling church services, school programs, and athletic events, and then the storm missed us entirely."

"Shush. We want to hear this."

"Heavy snow from fifteen to twenty plus inches is likely in the Twin Cities with higher snowfalls in the southern suburbs. Winds will be gusting up to fifty miles per hour, causing wind chills to be well below zero. At these temperatures exposed skin can be frostbitten in ten minutes. Expect blowing and drifting snow throughout the night. The blizzard warning continues through Monday evening. Avoid traveling unless it's an absolute necessity. If you do need to go out, allow plenty of time for your commute. Keep those kiddos safe -- and dog and cat owners, bring your pets inside. Stay tuned for school closings following the news at ten."

"Southern suburbs, that's us. I hope everyone has enough food."

"And booze," Karen said. "We might as well relax and hunker in."

Lynn looked out to Margaret's balcony where the light snow was accumulating. "It is beautiful. Like a snow globe. Magical really."

"Personally I could do without this kind of magic," Karen said.

"We should check on Susan; she's been hit hard with a cold. When I talked to her earlier, she sounded awful. Maybe one of us should take Dottie out before the weather gets too bad."

"I'll do it," Margaret said. "I'll bring her some *cassoulet* as well. It's not exactly chicken soup, but it does have chicken in it. Then I'll take Dottie out so Susan can stay warm and toasty."

"Make sure you get the poop before it gets buried in all the snow. I took her out in the last storm and had to ... "

"No need to explain. I get it," Margaret said as she started to put on layers of clothes.

* * *

Susan was watching TV and was fully aware of the blizzard warning, but she just didn't have the energy to care because she was coughing, sneezing, aching and thoroughly miserable. All she cared about was getting some sleep. Since this cold invaded, she hadn't been able to sleep more than a few hours at a time. Even with the standard, over-the-counter remedies, her body resisted sleep and her brain revved up like a NASCAR engine before a big race. So what did she do? She e-mailed Steve and the Dames at all hours of the day and night to chat. Well, mostly to complain. They were sympathetic, but she could tell they were tired of hearing about her symptoms. It was just a cold after all.

The doorbell rang and Susan, with Dottie by her side, answered the door to find Margaret looking like the Michelin man in her white down parka.

"Just thought I'd bring you some *cassoulet* and take Dottie out before the weather gets too bad. It's just beginning to get nasty. You look awful, by the way."

Susan's eyes were swollen; she needed a shower and she was wearing the same clothes she had on yesterday.

"Thanks, I really appreciate the food and the help. The 'awful' comment, not so much. I'll get her leash and a poop bag." Susan sneaked a peek at herself in the foyer mirror and Margaret was right: She looked awful.

Margaret bent down to scratch Dottie's belly. She'd never had a dog as a kid, but now that she'd gotten to know this likable mutt, she found she really liked dogs. And Dottie liked her, especially since Margaret frequently slipped her treats.

Like Margaret, Susan hadn't grown up around dogs, but when she reunited with Steve, he shared his love of dogs with her. With Steve's encouragement, she started snooping online. Then a trip to the local animal shelter and Susan was hooked. A silly, spotted black and white mutt with a polka-dot tail and eyebrows that relayed every feeling captured her heart. She made Susan laugh every day. Susan hadn't realized how lonely, depressed, and sad she was until Dottie became her beloved companion. Dottie got Susan out of her apartment and exercising, every day regardless of weather. Susan felt more optimistic and was the happiest she'd been in many years, even with a nasty cold. Dottie quickly became her dearest friend.

"I'll be right back. Just a quick walk and Dottie will be set until tomorrow morning."

"Oh wait, I'll get her coat and boots."

"Coat and boots, are you serious?"

"She's a short-haired dog and suffers from the cold, so I got her this fashionable red plaid jacket and matching boots. I think red is her color, don't you?"

"Doesn't she mind wearing doggy clothes?"

"At first she tried to shake the boots off, but now she associates her boots with her walk and tolerates them. She's always loved the coat, especially when people commented on how pretty she looks."

Margaret laughed at the thought of doggy fashion and doggy vanity.

"Come on, girl. It's time for your walk." Dottie looked fondly at Susan until Susan smiled and nodded. Then she wagged her assent and off they went.

Margaret and Dottie went out the front entrance to face the BIG ONE.

Snow was swirling like dust devils in the desert. In just an hour, at least three inches of snow had accumulated. The wind was bitter against Margaret's face, biting angrily against her woolen scarf. She could feel the cold through her thick down parka.

Walking down the driveway, she and Dottie hit a patch of ice covered with snow and Margaret went down face first, bracing her fall with her wrists. Her screams were swallowed by the wind. Dottie barked her dismay and ran off into the tempest.

CHAPTER 25

Just What the Doctor Ordered

After twenty minutes, Susan was getting worried. Margaret wasn't back from her brief walk with Dottie. Dressed in her heavy wool pea coat, a knit hat, and mittens she took her cell phone, plenty of tissues, and wheeled down to the apartment lobby and looked out into the storm. One look at the blizzard and she knew she needed help, so she phoned Karen, Lynn, and then Tom, anticipating Margaret might need some medical assistance. At least he would know what to do. He didn't answer so she left a voice mail and her cell number.

Lynn and Karen arrived in a flurry of excitement with scarves flying every which way. Lynn showed up in a black ski mask, her down coat an unbecoming lime green, looking a bit like an overstuffed couch planning a robbery. Karen was decked out in a multi- colored hand knit hat with earflap, a Dr. Who scarf wrapped around her neck several times and of course, the requisite Minnesota down jacket, this time in tasteful black. The coats and the accessories were ugly, but they were practical in below zero wind chills.

"Which way would Margaret and Dottie most likely head?" Lynn asked Susan. She was on high alert and all business.

"If I weren't so worried about them, I'd be laughing myself silly. Just look at you two!"

"You're confusing me with someone who gives a shit," Lynn responded in typical Lynn-speak. Most Minnesotans abandoned their vanity as well as their gender identities during a winter storm.

"When she and I walk Dottie together, we go toward the large perennial gardens, the one with the statue, so that would be a good place to start. I'm hoping she's just chatting with another dog walking resident," Susan said.

"Yeah right, a nice little chat in a raging blizzard. Come on, Karen, let's get a move on. We have to stick together. Take my hand." Bitterly cold air accompanied their departure. Susan was grateful she was still wearing her pea coat.

With heads down, Karen and Lynn headed out, hand in hand, toward the perennial gardens, the statue barely visible. In a matter of minutes the two Dames disappeared into the white, leaving Susan alone in the lobby.

Great, now I need to worry about them as well. Susan remembered stories about blizzards, the ones described in the *Little House on the Prairie* books, her childhood favorites. Then her mind flashed to her grandfather who was caught in the Armistice Day blizzard in November 1940. That storm killed forty-nine people. And who could forget the Halloween Blizzard of '91? Minnesota made national news with that one.

Get a grip, Girl. This isn't 1940 or 1991. People know better and have more accurate weather information. Dottie's microchipped and has ID on her collar. I'm so glad I put on her coat and boots. At least she'll be easy to spot .Damn. Margaret would have to be wearing a white coat.

Just then her cell phone rang. Tom explained that he had barely made it home from the hospital and wanted Susan to phone him once they'd found Margaret. Depending on injuries, they may need to phone an ambulance. Susan promised to check in with any news at all.

Time seemed to slow down, minutes seeming like hours. Several of her neighbors wandered into the lobby to chat about the storm and naturally they were curious about what had happened, Susan dressed as she was. She briefly explained the situation.

Susan was somewhat of a celebrity to them after the magazine article, and she was the only resident confined to a wheelchair. Walkers, however, were very popular. When they discovered what had happened, they were eager to join the search. Word spread fast in the community, and soon there were more than twenty residents out there, dressed like true Minnesotans, ready to battle the elements.

"Don't worry Ms. Waverly, we'll find them!" became the battle cry.

"Remember Dottie's wearing a red plaid coat and matching booties. Margaret's coat will blend in with the snow. Karen and Lynn, are out there as well. They headed toward the garden. Good luck and thanks everybody."

With that, her neighbors stormed out ready to rescue. Only Mrs. Simonson, the building's oldest resident, stayed behind to comfort and distract Susan. They could hear the calls for Margaret and Dottie getting fainter and fainter as the sound mixed with the wind.

Susan was sneezing, coughing, and generally miserable.

"Dear, could I get you something to drink? Tea perhaps? That's always good for a cold. Let's sit by the fire." Once they were comfortable, Mrs. Simonson dug around a large quilted bag to bring out a thermos and several mugs. She poured a steaming cup for Susan and one for herself. Then she reached into her bag and produced a small bottle of brandy and a bag of menthol cough drops. "I find that the brandy helps to steady my nerves. It's great for a cold as well. A dollop for you, my dear?"

Does she always travel with a thermos of tea and a bottle of brandy? What an odd little woman. Kind though. Susan nodded. *It might help me relax and stop this annoying cough.*

"A cough drop?"

"Thanks." Something about Mrs. Simonson reminded Susan of her grandmother.

158

Seeming to read Susan's mind, she again reached into her apparently bottomless bag and this time pulled out her iPad where she had stored hundreds of pictures of her grandchildren from babyhood to marriage. "Now let me show you my grandchildren."

Please. Somebody put me out of my misery.

While Mrs. Simonson was endlessly rhapsodizing about her beautiful family, Susan was thinking only of her dear friends, gone for over an hour. Normally that wouldn't have been a serious concern, but the blizzard with its dangerous wind-chills changed everything. Just the thought of something terrible happening to any of them made Susan cry.

"Now, now, dear. Everything will be all right. You'll see," the old lady said, as she patted Susan's hand. "Soon your sweet doggie and Mrs. Thompson will be safe and warm. And in a few days, when your cold has run its course, this will all be just a painful memory."

Just then they heard voices and saw two of their neighbors, one on each side of Margaret, opening the lobby door. Several others followed them into the warm. She was walking unsteadily, holding her arms close to her chest. She was very pale.

"How badly is she hurt?"

"She's definitely hurt her arms or wrists. When she slipped on the ice under the snow, she fell on her hands. We're lucky we saw her with all the snow; her white coat didn't help. She's such a little thing, I almost tripped over her."

"Where did you find her?"

"She was walking down the driveway toward the main road."

"Then that's where you should look for Dottie."

"This is all my fault. I am so sorry, Susan. When I fell, I dropped Dottie's leash and she ran off."

"In this weather it could have happened to anyone. We need to get you warm," Susan said.

They quickly got her sitting in one of the large upholstered chairs in front of the gas fireplace where she shivered uncontrollably. Lynn carefully removed Margaret's down mittens, but she whimpered in pain. When Lynn tried to get her coat off, she screamed.

"Here this should help." Mrs. Simonson offered her tea with a "dollop" of brandy. Dipping into her bag, she added another "dollop" or two or three to Margaret's tea.

"I think we should let her sit a bit, drink her tea and warm up," Mrs. Simonson said.

"Yes, that sounds lovely. I could use a little rest in front of the fire." With Mrs. Simonson's help, Margaret took a good swallow of tea. She grimaced slightly, but realized a shot or two of brandy couldn't hurt, so she drained her cup. Mrs. Simonson gave her a refill.

Susan wheeled over to where some of the neighbors were gathered. Many were still out looking for Dottie. "Any sign of my dog?"

"Sorry, but we'll keep looking after we warm up. We're taking fifteen minute shifts: fifteen in and fifteen out. We don't want anyone getting frostbite."

"Thank you so much. It's such a relief to have Margaret safe. Now if we can just find Lynn and Karen and my dog."

Just then the lobby door opened, letting in a poof of cold air. "Holy shit it's cold," Lynn said as she and Karen barged into the warmth. They stomped their feet, to dislodge the snow and to return circulation. After brushing snow off their coats and hats, they walked directly to Margaret and Mrs. Simonson. Margaret took one look at the black face mask and shivered.

"Take off the ninja mask," Karen said. "You're upsetting her."

"Sorry. Didn't mean to scare you. What happened? Are you okay?"

"I will be in a little while. I think I broke something in my wrists."

"Thank god, you're safe. We'll call Tom and he'll make everything better."

"He always does," Margaret said with a smile.

"Ladies, how about some fortified tea?" Again, the magic bag produced two more mugs and more brandy.

"When you're done being 'fortified,' we need to get her upstairs and comfortable. I've phoned Tom and he'll be here when he can. The roads are horrible, according to the TV and radio reports. We need to get her out of these clothes," Susan said. "We might need to cut off this very expensive coat." Margaret whimpered at the suggestion.

As Lynn and Karen were helping Margaret to her feet, the lobby door opened and they heard joyful whimpering.

As as soon as Dottie saw Susan, her rescuer dropped the leash and the mutt limped to Susan.

"You poor girl. Your feet must be freezing. Shake, Dottie." Susan took Dottie's paw. "I think she might have some frostbite on her feet."

"Look how polite and well-mannered that dog is," Mrs. Simonson said. "I wish my great grandkids were that well-behaved."

"She's such a good girl, aren't you, Dottie?" Susan bent down and scratched her behind her ears; Dottie licked Susan's face and then rolled on her back, exposing a polka-dot belly .

"Where did you find her?"

"She was on the side of the road about two blocks from here. I saw her red plaid coat.

She must have lost the boots when she ran away. She was so scared and cold."

"I don't care about the boots. I am so grateful she and Margaret were found. Thank you, everybody, for the help. Because of you, Margaret and Dottie have been saved from freezing to death."

Mrs. Simonson seized the moment: "How about a potluck party tomorrow? Since we'll all be housebound anyway, why don't we gather in the party room for supper?" The crowd seemed to think this was a good idea. "Everybody bring something. It will be fun. We can celebrate Margaret and Dottie's rescue and being among such good people. Anyone wanting to help organize, stick around a few minutes and we'll pull this together. Over here, friends."

"Well, I suppose a potluck might not be such a bad idea, considering the restaurant will most likely be closed. Damn weather! That Mrs. Simonson is something else," Karen said as they helped Margaret on the elevator.

"I hope she doesn't bring her fortified tea. It was awful," Lynn said.

"I thought it was just what the doctor ordered," Margaret said, giggling.

CHAPTER 26

"Always Look on the Bright Side of Life."

Susan took Dottie back to the apartment to minister to Dottie's frostbitten feet while Lynn and Karen got Margaret back to her apartment, ready to perform surgery on Margaret's $500 designer Canadian goose down coat.

"Where do you keep your kitchen shears?"

"Not my beautiful coat," Margaret said. "Let's try again to get the coat off. I've had Mrs. Simonson's fortified tea which was almost all brandy. I'm currently feeling no pain."

"Okay, but if it's too much, we'll use the scissors. Ready?"

"Just do it."

Lynn and Karen carefully extricated Margaret from her precious coat with considerable discomfort for all involved.

"Hooah!" Lynn and Karen yelled in unison when the coat came off.

"'Hooah!' What's that about?" Margaret said.

"Just a voice from our past. Long story, for another time," Karen said. "Now we've got to survey the damage."

When they pulled up the sleeves of her sweater, they were shocked at the considerable swelling and discoloration of her wrists and her fingers.

"Little sausages; that's what my fingers look like! Thank goodness I'd already taken off my rings before I took Dottie outside."

"'Always look on the bright side of life,'" Lynn said as she broke into song.

"Apparently I wasn't the only one drinking Mrs. Simonson's brew," Margaret said, laughing.

"Too bad we don't have *The Life of Brian* to watch since we're blizzard bound. It would be a nice diversion," Karen said.

"Better than the Simonson potluck," Lynn said. "Depending on the food, of course."

The Dames were convinced Margaret had broken both her wrists. Now they were waiting for their diagnosis to be confirmed by Tom, but since the roads were impassable they had to "make do" with a phone call.

"Describe her wrists and arms ... she's probably broken them... Give her extra strength Tylenol every four hours and make sure her wrists are elevated. An ice pack would help keep the swelling down. I'll try to get there as soon as I can. She needs to go to the hospital for x-rays."

"Be safe. She needs you," Karen said.

The Dames followed the doctor's orders, got her out of her clothes and into a warm nightgown. They helped her wash her face, brush her teeth, and tucked her into bed, shoring up both arms with pillows.

"This dependence is embarrassing. Good Lord, I even need help using the bathroom. Heaven help me if I have a bowel movement."

"My mother used to say, 'You're lucky if you have five wipe-your-butt friends,'" Lynn said.

"Guess that makes me lucky indeed, as long as Tom isn't on the list." The Dames laughed.

"Would you like your wig removed?" Margaret nodded, too tired to object. The drugs were beginning to work. The Dames removed her wig, displaying very short curls.

"I love your hair just as is. It's very becoming," Karen said. "You're still very beautiful even without your wig and makeup."

"Thank you, but I don't agree. I wish there was some treatment for thinning hair, besides wearing wigs. Getting old is very demeaning. I want to retain as much of my dignity as I can for as long as I can."

"Don't we all," Lynn said, though Lynn was notoriously undignified.

"Are you in a lot of pain?"

"Between the brandy and the Tylenol, I'm moderately comfortable, as long as I don't move. Speaking of brandy, would you raid my liquor cabinet for tomorrow's potluck gathering. Just a small way to say thank-you."

"Consider it done," Lynn said.

"We'll stay the night. Here is the bell you used when you broke your foot and ankle. Ring if you need anything. I'll wake you in four hours for two more Tylenol and see if you need anything."

"I owe you two. You've been my guardian angels twice in six months. I don't know that I deserve such devoted, or to quote your mom 'wipe-my-butt friends.'"

"I know you'd do the same for us," Lynn said as she kissed Margaret on the forehead.

"Sweet dreams, Dear Friend."

Once they had retired to the living room, they poured themselves a generous glass of red wine and put their feet up. The snow continued to swirl and drift, obliterating the deck furniture.

"Isn't this fireplace a godsend? I use mine all the time in the winter."

"Me too," Lynn said, taking another sip of wine. She paused, taking in the storm and all its beauty. "Did you notice how thin she was?"

"Sure did. And I'm concerned about the number of broken bones in the last few months as well."

"When did Margaret start wearing wigs?"

"Good question."

"I think it was a couple of years ago after she went on that month long vacation to Mexico. I figured she was having more "work" done and needed time to heal. She's a very private person and this latest misadventure must be terribly difficult for her. She'd never want us to see her so vulnerable."

"Are you thinking what I'm thinking?"

"Cosmetic surgery or an affair with a hot tamale?"

"No, I'm thinking it wasn't cosmetic surgery or the hot tamale—that maybe it was something more serious."

"Karen, you always go to the dark place. Lighten up. Margaret has always been tiny. We shrink when we get older. I know she has osteoporosis. That would certainly account for the broken bones."

"You're probably right, Lynn."

"When Tom gets here, we can share our concerns and ask him a few questions."

"Suddenly I'm exhausted. Must be the wine, the brandy, the fireplace, the snow. Why don't you take the couch and I'll take Margaret's leather chair? I don't know if I can sleep quite yet, but go ahead. I'm content to stare at the snow and the fire. Makes me think of 'Fire and Ice" that poem by Robert Frost. Remember it?"

Lynn's snores answered the question.

> Some say The world will end in fire,
>   Some say in ice.
> From what I've tasted of desire.
>   I hold with those who favor fire.
> But if it had to perish twice,
>   I think I know enough of hate.
> To say that for destruction ice.
>   Is also great. And would suffice.

I'm amazed I remembered that. My 11th grade English teacher would be proud.

After an hour or so of 'fire and ice' gazing, Karen's eyes got heavy and she finally fell asleep.

* * *

Around three in the morning both Lynn and Karen were awakened by the entrance buzzer and Tom's loud demand to be admitted.

"Lynn, Karen, let me in. I'm freezing."

"Hold your horses," Lynn said, rubbing her neck. "I should never sleep on a couch. I always wake up with a stiff neck and hair that sticks up on one side."

"Quit whining and let the good doctor in. I'll start the coffee. Leave the door open a crack."

"Aye, aye, Captain." Lynn gave Karen her famous one fingered salute. After following her commanding officer's instructions, Lynn headed off to use the bathroom and to check on Margaret who was still asleep, but wouldn't be for long.

Karen heard a gentle knock on the open door. "Is she still sleeping?" Tom said, standing in the foyer, looking like a snowman.

"Wow, that was fast," Karen said.

"Yeah, I can move when I'm worried."

"Take off your boots and shake your coat off in the hallway. We don't want puddles on the wood floor."

"You sound like my mother." Tom grumbled, but did as he was told. Then he went directly to Margaret's bedroom. Lynn left to give them some privacy.

"He certainly seems to know his way around," Karen said, raising her eyebrows with the implication.

"Of course he does. They've been fuck buddies for quite awhile."

Karen cringed slightly at the language. "Too much information."

"My, my, aren't we prudish tonight."

"Guess I'm just tired."

"Don't you ever long for sex?" Lynn asked, ignoring her pal's verbal and nonverbal cues.

"Not so much any more, but I do long for someone to hold my hand and cuddle once in awhile. I would like to come home and have someone be truly interested in me and my life. I guess I just crave intimacy, you know. Maybe I need a dog."

"Don't we do that for you?"

"Yeah, but you don't hold my hand and cuddle."

"Okay," Lynn said as she went to Karen and held her hand. "Now do you feel better?" Karen laughed and gave her good friend a hug.

"You're the next best thing to a fuck buddy," Lynn said and they both laughed. "Speaking of fuck buddies. Shall we?" Lynn nodded at the bedroom. Since the door was open, they felt it was their duty to eavesdrop.

"Come on in, you two. I know you're out there listening," Margaret said to her good friends.

"You know us well," Lynn said.

"How did you sleep?" Karen asked.

"Pretty well, considering. How about you?"

"My neck is stiff, but I'm fine. Except for my hair."

"Lynn, has anyone told you how vain you are about your hair?"

"You have—about a million times."

"How about some coffee? I just made some. And maybe some toast?" Karen looked at Tom and Margaret.

"Have any eggs?" Tom grinned. He was holding Margaret's hand.

"See, that's what I'm talking about," Karen said, nodding in the couple's direction.

"Come on, Karen. Let's give them some privacy."

"I like mine scrambled." Tom winked.

CHAPTER 27

Blasted Blizzard

While Lynn and Karen were seeing to Margaret, Susan was attending to Dot and her frostbitten feet.

As soon as they got into the apartment after the rescue, Susan turned on the fireplace and Dot immediately limped to her very expensive doggy bed and curled up in front of the fire. Susan knew that she couldn't take Dot to the vet's in this weather, so she went to her computer to research treatment and found that her Wi-Fi wasn't working.

"Damn weather," Susan said more to herself than Dot, but Dot wagged her tail as if she agreed with the assessment. "I seem to remember that you're supposed to warm frostbitten hands and feet in warm, not hot water. And I also remember that you're not supposed to rub them. Good thing you had your coat and your boots, at least for awhile. Isn't that right, sweet girl?" Dot's polka dot tail thumped on her doggy bed.

Susan went to the bathroom to prepare warm compresses for Dot. By the time she got back, Dot was sleeping soundly. She picked up each foot and held it tenderly in her hand, warming it before applying the warm, moist towel.

"I think you're going to be just fine, sweet friend." Susan left Dottie to her slumber and went to the phone to call about Margaret. After the update, Susan acknowledged her exhaustion, but instead of sleeping in her bed, she chose the comfortable sectional, so she could be near Dottie. After a swig of night time cold medicine, Susan feel into a deep, peaceful sleep.

The Dames and Tom awakened the next day to absolute silence, the world outside void of any noise, the cars buried in snow, the sidewalks impossible to navigate, the roads totally unusable.

When they turned on the news, newscasters advised no travel unless it was an absolute emergency. It wasn't until nearly eleven that the clean-up began, and then the noise was as accentuated as the prior silence. Plows, snow blowers, even snowmobilers were out in full force. The Dames looked out on the river and saw cross country skiers and snow-mobilers enjoying the wintry conditions.

"I never understood why anyone would want a snow-mobile until this blizzard. And now they make perfect sense," Lynn said, drinking her third cup of coffee. "This way we could go to lunch, no problem. And maybe some of the employees in our restaurant could get to work."

Lynn and Karen had helped Margaret get ready for the day, choosing warm, loose-fitting clothes. Tom was outside trying to find his car in the abundance of drifts; he had the sense to dig up to the license plates until he finally located his SUV. He didn't want to spend hours digging out some other guy's car, most likely a visitor's because the residents' vehicles were safely in the underground parking area.

Tom looked up from shoveling to see a large pink lump of down, wearing a white fur hat of indeterminable origins with matching furry mittens, waddling in his direction and carrying a large quilted bag. The only indication of gender was the coat's color.

As it got closer, it was clearly an elderly she. "Could you please help me after you find your car? I know mine is in here somewhere and I have to get to the grocery store before the big party tonight."

"Excuse me?" Tom said as he continued to shovel out his car. "Do I know you?"

"I don't think we've formally met, but I've sure seen you plenty of times. You're Margaret's doctor friend. I'm Mrs. Simonson from the fourth floor. I helped out last night when Margaret and the dog went missing."

"Yes, thank you so much for helping. I'm trying to get Margaret to the hospital for x-rays, as soon as possible."

"Of course, I understand. I'll just have to hire someone to help. I am just an old woman on a fixed income." She sighed and looked deliberately pathetic. "If you're cold and need a bracer, I have hot tea in my bag."

"I've heard about your tea, Mrs. Simonson, and if I weren't in such a hurry to get Margaret to the hospital, I would gladly help you with your car. If you don't mind my asking, why wasn't your car in the underground parking area?"

"We only get one space and this is my extra vehicle, a new Mustang with ecoboost, whatever that means. I admired Margaret's car and decided I needed one of those wild mustangs. Would you like to see a picture of Maggie?" Mrs. Simonson rummaged around in her bag for her iPad.

Old woman on a fixed income, my ass. That must be some fixed income! And now I have to see pictures of her sports car named after my girlfriend. Help!

"Why don't you take your other car? Far less hassle."

"And far less fun."

"Mrs. Simonson, there you are," one of the elderly residents yelled as he trudged through the snow. "We need your help setting up for tonight's potluck celebration." He helped Mrs. Simonson back into the building where she was, no doubt, showing everyone pictures of her grandchildren and her car.

Thank God I didn't have to drink her spiked tea or see her pictures.

Tom continued to clean off his vehicle. The parking lot had been plowed, but the plow had pushed even more snow onto the vehicles. Even though he had arrived at three in the morning, his car was still buried, thanks to the plow.

Fortunately, he had packed a snow shovel and kitty litter to help with traction in case he got stuck. He hoped the freeways would be clear by the time he managed to escape the parking lot. Thank heavens his Forester had four wheel drive. After an hour of shoveling, his car was ready to go.

He phoned Margaret to tell her to meet him in front of the entrance in about ten minutes.

Margaret, her coat draped over her shoulders, was waiting in the lobby with Karen when Tom drove up. Karen held onto Margaret as she gingerly got into Tom's Forester.

"Call when you know anything and be careful. Take your time."

"Will do. Valuable cargo," Tom smiled at Margaret.

* * *

Six hours later Tom and Margaret returned to the apartment. Margaret, looking pale and fragile, had both wrists in splints.

"We need to get her back in bed. Fortunately, she has only fractured her left wrist; the right is just badly sprained. We'll cast the left wrist once the swelling decreases, probably in a few days. Meanwhile, she'll need to ice both wrists, keep them elevated, and take the same pain killers as yesterday. I can stay with her until tomorrow morning when I need to get back to work. Then it's going to be up to you."

"How long will she need us twenty-four-seven?" Lynn asked.

"Do you have a hot date I should know about?" Karen stared in Lynn's direction.

"In my dreams. Just wondering if I should cancel a few things."

"You should be able to take shifts once she has her cast. That makes all the difference in mobility. She'll feel more confident and less scared about doing more damage. She will need someone to drive her to her doctor's appointments. Maybe you could employ Tiffany again."

172

"She's going to school full time and working about fifteen hours a week at the salon. I doubt she'll be available."

"In the meantime, let's take it a day at a time. Together we'll work it out. There are four of us. I can take the night shift, if you ladies can handle the days."

"We'll manage, I'm sure," Karen said.

"We wanted to ask a few questions about Margaret's general health. Like why is she breaking so many bones? And why is she losing weight?"

"I'm afraid I can't answer those questions. You'll have to ask her."

"Doctor/patient confidentiality I suppose. I watch those shows on TV. It's all BS if you ask me."

"Those are the rules," Tom said, trying to placate Lynn.

"So now you're her doctor? I thought you couldn't date a patient. That's why you referred her to someone else when she broke her foot and ankle." Lynn continued pushing.

"This is just temporary. Her orthopedist was unavailable today because of the weather. When she's able to get her cast, she will see her former doctor. Does that meet with your approval, Lynn?"

"I guess," Lynn said. "So once she gets her cast you can talk to us like a regular person?"

"As long as it's okay with Margaret, Now that that's settled, let's see if we can get her to eat something. There is a party going on downstairs and a very full buffet table. Check it out—nothing too heavy or spicy for Margaret, but I'm game for anything."

"I'm sure you are," Lynn said under her breath. "Let's grab some containers, Karen, and get us some food."

CHAPTER 28

News Flash!

As soon as Lynn and Karen entered the party room, they were swarmed by curious neighbors wanting to know how Margaret and Dot the Dog were doing.

Equipped with a full kitchen, a gas fireplace, lounge chairs, comfortable sofas, and a large table where the food and beverages were displayed, the room was perfect for a gratitude banquet. Both Margaret and Susan had donated wine and hard liquor as a thank-you to their neighbors.

The large room was decorated with white lights and leftover poinsettias from Christmas. One of the neighbors was playing bad piano bar music on the community piano and several of the women were gathered around singing. Their neighbors were obviously enjoying the libations or as Margaret called them "liquid sweaters."

Just as they were explaining Margaret's medical condition, Susan and Dottie made their appearance. Suddenly, everyone shifted their attention to the newcomers, leaving Lynn and Karen to fend for themselves.

"I guess we're now chopped liver," Lynn said as their neighbors abandoned them for more interesting company.

"Great, let's raid the buffet table before all the good stuff's gone." The Dames took their containers and started loading up with a variety of pasta, vegetable and fruit salads, chicken stuffed enchiladas, chicken wings, barbecued meatballs, smoked salmon, tapioca pudding, and a wide variety of cookies and bars.

"That should be enough to feed four people," Lynn said as she crammed fresh fruit into a gallon sized freezer bag.

Just then Mrs. Simonson buzzed past Lynn and Karen on her way to the guest of honor: Dot the Dog. "There's that sweet, well-behaved, smart pup," Mrs. Simonson said. "I have a treat for you, Miss Dottie." She reached into her magic quilted bag and pulled out a box of large Milk Bones. She also pulled out a bottle of brandy, and toddled over to add it to the beverage table.

"How does she do that? It reminds me of Mary Poppins's suitcase."

"Carpet bag."

"What about the carpet?"

"Mary Poppins carried a carpet bag not a suitcase. And you should consider adjusting your hearing aids."

"What? Can't hear you in all this racket. Let's hit the road before we have to make more small talk or look at pictures of Mrs. Simonson's grandchildren," Karen said. The Dames waved at Susan as they hurried from the noisy celebration, arms laden with goodies.

"Meals on Wheels at your service," Karen yelled as she entered Margaret's silent apartment. "Anyone home?"

"We're in the bedroom," Tom yelled.

"Surprise, surprise," Karen said, rolling her eyes.

They stacked their stash in the kitchen and went to join the couple.

"I've got salads, casseroles that I can heat up in the microwave, appetizers and desserts. We're here to take your orders. For you?" Lynn said as she noticed Margaret's red eyes.

"Are you okay, Margaret?"

"I'm okay. I just don't like being so dependent on my friends. I want to be able to take care of myself and get my own damn food. Just get me something you think I might like. Nothing too spicy." She stopped to blow her nose and wipe her eyes. "Sorry to be so cranky."

"Anger is a good thing. I get it, but until you get that arm cast you're going to have to tolerate our ugly mugs."

"Speak for yourself, Karen. My mug is only moderately ugly."

"Tom? Your order?"

"I'll have what she's having." All the Dames laughed at that, remembering that famous quote from their favorite movie.

"Give us about ten minutes and we'll be back."

When they were just outside the door, Lynn heard Tom ask, "When are you going to tell them, Margaret?"

"When it's closer to the time."

"Did you hear that?" Lynn was whispering.

"I didn't hear a thing, including what you just whispered. Remember my hearing aids need to be fine-tuned, as you so often remind me."

As soon as they got to the kitchen, Lynn blabbed. Notorious for being unable to keep a secret, Lynn seldom made it to Christmas without giving her kids, grandkids, and friends their gifts. Sometimes even Santa delivered early. And gossip went in her ears and out her mouth in seconds.

"I knew it. They're getting married. It will probably be a spring wedding; I just love spring weddings—the flowers, the colors, the promise of happiness. Who do you think will be maid of honor? If you're divorced are you a maid or a matron?"

"I could care less. Generally I hate weddings; I've had three and look how they turned out. The promise of happiness—what a crock."

"Well, I think they'll be very happy. He's kind of growing on me. At our age it's good to have a doctor close by. I always wanted to marry a veterinarian and instead I married a cardiologist with no heart. Tom seems to have a big heart; at least I hope he does. I can hardly wait to tell Susan. I wonder if she's back yet from the party. I'll call and see."

"Aren't you going to help with the food?"

"Give me a minute, Karen. I have important news to share."

"You don't even know if that's what Tom meant. Don't you think you should make sure it's true before you blab to Susan?"

"What else could he mean? Nah, it's a wedding. I have a special sense for these things," Lynn said as she took out her cell phone to call Susan.

"Like you predicted that Susan would fall for Bruce, the dog walker. How did that work out, huh?"

"She did hire him to walk Dottie. That's something, even if she didn't fall for his obvious charms. I think he's hot."

"Well, maybe you should pursue Bruce, even though he's thirty years younger. Maybe he likes chubby cat collectors," Karen said, laughing at the thought of Bruce walking a couple of Lynn's fat cats.

"Are you calling me chubby? Or my cats?"

"Both actually."

Lynn tried Susan again. "Not answering."

"Of course she's not answering. She's still at the potluck; you have the attention of a fly at a picnic."

"Right. I forgot. I'll leave a voice message: Call ASAP. I've got news!"

CHAPTER 30

Timing is Everything

After an hour at the potluck, Susan was exhausted; these kinds of gatherings drained her energy on the best of days, but with a nasty cold, she was running on empty. Dottie, on the other hand, was enjoying every pat, every kind word, and every tasty morsel coming her way, soaking up the attention like the love addict she was.

"Come on, Dottie. It's time for us to go. Thanks again for yesterday. It's such a comfort to know we're living in such a kind and generous community. Enjoy the party, everyone."

Dottie wagged her tail and Susan started coughing.

"You need to go back to bed, dear," Mrs. Simonson said, patting Dottie on the head. "You too, Susan."

"Let's stop by Margaret's and see how she is," Susan said as she got on the elevator. Just the mention of Margaret's name made Dot wag her tail. It was because of the treats she imagined coming from Margaret. Dot would look at Margaret with those sad puppy eyes until she gave in and shared her food.

As soon as they knocked on Margaret's door, Lynn answered, whispering, "I've been trying to call you for the last half hour. You won't believe what I found out tonight."

"I was sort of busy at the potluck. Why the whispers?"

Lynn took Susan to the kitchen where she explained about overhearing Tom and Margaret talking about a possible wedding.

"Are you sure they're planning their wedding? It could be something like a vacation or buying a time share?"

"Tom said,'When are you going to tell them?' He's obviously talking about us. Then Margaret answered, 'When it's closer to the time.' That doesn't sound like a vacation to me.'"

"I told her to keep her mouth shut until she knew for sure, but that was like telling her to eat one French fry or watch one re-run of *Fixer Upper*—just not going to happen."

"Well, I'll just go into the bedroom and ask them. I believe in the direct approach."

"Don't. She'll just think I'm a snoopy, gossipy old lady."

"But you are a snoopy, gossipy old lady."

"Well, fuck me. I'm staying here." Susan and Karen laughed because Lynn misused the F bomb once again.

"I don't think I can face them right now. I'd be too embarrassed. I wouldn't want to be accused of jumping to conclusions."

Karen snorted, "Like the time you thought your daughter was pregnant when she had the stomach flu. Or the time you..."

"Okay, okay, so I occasionally jump to conclusions, but I wasn't the only one. You started knitting baby clothes the day after I told you."

"*Touche.*"

Susan left to confront Margaret, but she returned after only a few minutes.

"Wow, that was fast."

"When I looked in the room, Margaret was crying. Tom was holding her and it seemed inappropriate to interrupt. I'll wait until tomorrow when she's feeling better, more like herself. Timing is everything. What's with all the tears anyway?"

"She's in pain, frustrated and angry at being laid up— again. She's had a tough few days. Can't say I blame her. "

"I get it," Susan said.

"I'm sure you do, considering all you've been through," Karen said and Lynn nodded in agreement.

"Susan, I've been thinking that Margaret and Tom should tell us their news when they're ready and in their own way. I think I might have been jumping to conclusions. Whatever the story, it's not my story to tell."

Karen looked at her friend in utter astonishment. "Wow. Now that's something to celebrate—Lynn's showing some restraint about spreading gossip. Impressive, girlfriend. What changed your mind?"

"Both of you made some good points. I have jumped to conclusions in the past, and I like to think I've learned something, so, as much as I hate to admit it, you were right. I would like you two to keep this between us. Promise?"

"Promise," Karen said.

"I'll keep your secret," Susan said. "You're not going to make us link pinkies or anything are you?"

"Thanks. I appreciate that."

"Sure you don't want anything to eat? There's still a lot of food here and some of it is pretty good." Lynn, as always, covered her discomfort by changing the subject.

"No thanks. I'll heat up some chicken noodle soup, take my cold medicine, and go to bed. Mrs. Simonson took Dottie out for a brief walk so we're good."

"Hope you're feeling better soon," Karen said.

"Thanks. I'll check in tomorrow."

When Susan and Dottie got back to her apartment, she phoned Steve, updating him on her evening. They had a good laugh at Lynn's expense. Before she said goodnight she said, "About your proposal, I think we should go for it." Dottie was snoozing on her bed in front of the fireplace. Susan poured herself a red wine and contemplated her future. Life was good.

CHAPTER 31

Mexican Spring

Two months later

The Dames were once again gathered in Margaret's apartment for another round of "Pop Goes the Weasel." Because of the busy holiday season and Margaret's injuries, they hadn't gotten around to nominating another client after Bob Miller.

It was the end of March and winter was holding spring hostage which meant the Dames were feeling a bit claustrophobic and crabby, typical for most Minnesotans anxious for green grass, lilacs, and pleasant walks. They tried to moderate their moods with fresh flowers and lots of wine.

Susan was engaged to Steve again, Margaret was still dating the handsome, very nice doctor, Karen was continuing to knit complicated shawls and afghans for anybody who expressed even the remotest interest, and Lynn was enjoying cheesecake and croissants with gusto. She had to euthanize a few more cats due to old age, so she ate to help ease her grief. In other words, it was business as usual, or so they thought.

"Ladies, it's time for another nomination." The Dames paused momentarily in their gossip to listen. "Only this time the process will be slightly different. There will be only one nominee." The gossip stopped and they looked at their beloved friend with renewed interest. Margaret now had their full attention. She was still impeccably groomed, but her color was off and she had lost weight. Instead of standing, Margaret was sitting in her leather recliner.

"Does that mean you're the only one who can nominate because I found another local who could use extermination." Lynn made a gesture like slitting her throat.

"Just be patient, Lynn, and I'll answer the question."

"I'm not sure I understand."

"I liked our nomination process just like it was."

"Why the change?"

Only Susan remained without questions.

"Well, this is hard, so bear with me, Ladies. As you know Tom and I are friends."

"Friends with benefits," Lynn said, grinning. *Here come the wedding plans. I just knew it.*

"Nice euphemism, Lynn," Karen said. And then Karen whispered loud enough for everyone to hear, "Lynn usually says 'fuck buddies.'"

"Whatever term you want to use is okay with me. At my age, I don't much care what you call it. Tom has been a godsend. He's been loving, caring, and totally unselfish. When I broke my foot and ankle, Tom was the attending physician. He was the one looking at the x-rays. Remember when he wanted to talk to me alone? And you two," Margaret said, pointing at Karen and Lynn, "assumed it was because he wanted to ask me out. But it was more than that. He was concerned about what he saw on the x-ray."

Now the Dames were totally focused on their dear friend.

"Apparently my breast cancer had metastasized into my bones." The Dames gasped in unison.

"Breast cancer?"

"When did you have breast cancer?"

"Why didn't you tell us?"

"What the hell is going on?"

"I must confess: I haven't been totally honest with you.

Do you remember when I went away for a month a few summers ago? I told you I was going on vacation—to Mexico."

"I thought you were having a face lift or an eye lift, something cosmetic," Karen said.

"And I thought you might be having an affair," Lynn said, slightly ashamed.

"Either would have been acceptable, though I'd vote for the affair," Margaret said, smiling. "Unfortunately, it wasn't anything remotely pleasant. I had a lumpectomy, a minor procedure to remove a small tumor in my right breast. It was cancer, but the oncologist at Mayo thought it was contained. To be on the safe side she suggested chemo."

"Ah... that explains the wigs," Lynn said. "So you stayed in Rochester all that time?"

"Yes, it made more sense to stay there, so I could eliminate all the commuting. I didn't want to inconvenience you. I lied to all of you and told you I was on vacation in Mexico."

"But we would have been happy to help," Karen said.

"I know that now. You've all been so supportive with your company and your help, but back then I just felt this was too personal. You know how I am about my privacy and how I hate to be dependent on anyone, let alone dear friends. If I've learned anything, it's how to ask for help when I need it."

"Are you going to try chemo again?" Susan asked.

"No. Some people breeze through chemo, but I wasn't one of them. I actually had one round of treatments, but I couldn't take the side effects. Plus, I lost all my hair. And you know how vain I am about my hair. So I terminated chemo, knowing full well the cancer could return. And it has. So now the cancer has spread to my bones. That's why every time I fall I break something. I've seen the x-rays; my bones look like a honeycomb. My prognosis is grim: stage four and terminal. The doctors are hesitant to say how long I have, but they have told me to put my affairs in order. Tom will be there with me and I know you will be too."

The Dames were silent except for Lynn who started blubbering uncontrollably.

"Does that mean you aren't planning your wedding?" Lynn said between hiccups. Karen put her arm around Lynn's shoulders. Margaret wasn't deterred.

"No, Lynn, there won't be a wedding, at least not mine."

"But Tom asked you about when you were going to tell us. I heard him the day of the gratitude party."

"He probably did. My mind's a bit fuzzy about that day. I was referring to my diagnosis, not my wedding. Sorry to disappoint you."

At that, Lynn tried to swallow her sobs and listen, but gulps and snorts still escaped. When Lynn cried, it was ugly.

"I am a firm believer in maintaining control over my own destiny. I know that when I'm no longer able to walk, read, enjoy good food and drink with my friends, maintain my physical appearance without help, generally enjoy life that I want to control when I die. I don't want to languish in pain and ugliness. But most of all I don't want to be a burden. That's where you folks and Tom come in. I want your help when the time is right and I'll know when that is."

"Are we going to talk about this like we do with other clients?" Karen asked.

Susan, who had remained relatively quiet up to this point said, "I'm going to be honest with you, Margaret. After my accident, I felt exactly like you. I wanted to die. I thought my life was over. I'd lost Steve and the use of my legs. More importantly I lost all sense of self worth. Over time and with the help of friends like you I regained my will to live, but it was a long process. And you don't have that time. I understand where you're coming from."

"Well, I don't," Lynn blurted. "Are you asking us to 'put you down' like I've had to do with three cats in the last six months?"

"I'm asking that you help me 'put myself down.' I am the Closer, after all. Now do you understand?"

The Dames went absolutely silent at the thought. Margaret endured the silence for a few minutes and then she went on with her plan.

"I want to make this as pleasant as possible, so we're going on a final girls' getaway at my expense. We're going to Puerto Aventuras, Mexico for the last two weeks in April and the first two weeks in May.

I've rented a beautiful handicap accessible home right on the beach. So clear your calendars, Ladies. Tom will be with us in case we need him, but he's agreed to stay out of our way. I want us to spend quality time together away from this cold, dreary weather. Mexico will be our spring and my summer. We'll laugh, drink, and reminisce about our lives. We'll be honest, open, and loving, but most of all, we're going to have fun. So let's get started early. Karen, there's a pitcher of margaritas in the fridge in case anyone wants to get in the mood."

The Dames were silent.

"I think I speak for all of us: We need some time to process all of this. I'm going to pass on the drinks," Karen said.

"Keep them in the fridge. Maybe tomorrow?" Lynn said.

"I understand; I've given you a lot to think about. Let's say five tomorrow. A Mexican Happy Hour. Karen, will you please get my walker from my bedroom?"

"A walker?" Lynn whispered to Susan.

"I heard you, Lynn. I'll be using a walker from now on. Soon it will be a wheelchair, so get used to the new normal. Thanks for everything. You've been kind and generous friends. I love all of you. So until tomorrow."

One by one the Dames gave Margaret a very gentle hug. Susan was the last to leave. When she went to Margaret she said, "I get it."

"I know you do. Thank you."

CHAPTER 32

Guacamole Anyone?

As soon as Lynn, Karen, and Susan left, they started talking and arranged to meet in Susan's apartment the next morning for some serious debriefing. They each needed to process the information privately in their own way: Lynn went home to cry with her kitties, Karen to the TV to binge-watch more *Property Brothers* make-overs, and Susan to her computer to research doctor-assisted suicide or death with dignity.

* * *

"Can you believe how upbeat Margaret was? She's arranging her own death, for Christ sake and she's got margaritas in the fridge. I just don't get it. I'd be crying my eyes out," Lynn said.

"You were crying your eyes out," Karen said.

"So, is that so hard to understand?"

"Not really. I saved the crying until I got home. After a few stupid TV shows, I remembered something I read in a magazine while waiting in the doctor's office for my yearly physical. It was about teenagers contemplating suicide. Once they'd made up their minds, they felt all upbeat and happy. That confused their friends because they mistakenly assumed their friend was getting better. Maybe that's what's happening with Margaret."

"From what I've read, once people who are terminally ill get the medication for their death, they feel much better because they are in control. If the pain gets unbearable, they can end it. It's all very comforting for them," Susan said.

"And what about their loved ones? Is it comforting for them?"

"Good question. Most of the information I've found focuses on the terminally ill patient."

"I get not wanting to suffer. But now there's palliative care that eases suffering and hospice care that allows people to die with some kind of dignity. It's not like there are no options. When my dad was dying, he just stopped eating and drinking. It took nearly a week. Now that was hard to watch," Lynn said, her nurse's training beginning to surface.

"Wouldn't it have been kinder if your father had had the option to end his suffering? To say nothing of his family's having to watch," Susan said. Lynn didn't respond.

"Back to Margaret ... She's probably in shock, feeling like this is really happening to someone else. I know I've felt that way when my life was in crisis. The difference being Margaret's pain is physical and that pain is only going to worsen. Can you imagine breaking bones with an accidental bump? Even sitting might eventually get dangerous.

"She's so thin. Not like me with my big ol' booty."

"And I wonder how Tom is reacting to all of this. It's obvious how much he loves her. From what Margaret has said, he is willing to help with the actual event. I'm assuming he will provide the medication. If he gets the meds in Minnesota, is he breaking the law? Minnesota doesn't have a Physician Assisted Dying law," Lynn said.

"I have no idea," Susan said. "As a doctor, Tom has lots of access to prescription drugs; I doubt getting the drugs will be a problem. By the way, only California, Colorado, Oregon, Vermont, and Washington have the Death with

Dignity law and they require residency or waiting periods between completing the required forms. Again Margaret doesn't have that time," Susan said.

"That explains the Mexico plans. By renting a house, she will have isolated herself. I doubt that anyone, even Mexican authorities, would question her death, considering her condition. Who knows how bad she'll be by the time we get there."

"Let's get to the nitty gritty. How exactly do we help her?" Karen asked.

"Before we have that discussion, shouldn't we take a vote like we've done with our other clients? Speaking of 'other clients,' you don't suppose Margaret has told Tom?"

"She wouldn't do that. We're sworn to secrecy," Susan said. "Now if it were you, Lynn, I'd be worried."

"Okay, so I tend to overshare. I admit I've blabbed a few secrets, so big fuckin' deal," Lynn said. "Enough with the blather; let's vote."

"Okay. Who's in favor of helping Margaret? Raise your hands." Karen and Susan raised their hands.

"I see we haven't quite convinced you, Lynn. Why not?"

"It just seems so cold and calculated. She's our good friend, not some sleazy stranger who has done evil things. She's a good person."

"Who is suffering and her suffering will only get worse."

"And what about the all-expenses-paid trip to Mexico? A reward for helping to knock her off? I can't wrap my brain around any of this. We get to euthanize our dear friend — what a trip. I mean that literally."

"Technically it wouldn't be euthanasia because Margaret, with our help, would be doing it, not the doctor," Susan said.

"What kind of doctor would help someone kill themselves?" Lynn asked.

"A compassionate one?" Karen answered.

"I mean how do you even help someone do themselves in?"

"I've been doing some research and I found out quite a

bit of information." Susan described various death cocktails and the time it takes for the drugs to work.

"So does 'helping' mean we mix the cocktail and hand it to her? Then give her a tasty chaser?"

"There was a scene in *House of Cards* where Claire gives her mother an overdose of morphine, at her mother's request. I thought at the time that it would be a pleasant way to go. Just float away. Morphine overdose is another possibility. I think Tom will probably see to the specifics," Susan continued.

"Who will take care of my furbabies while I'm on this so-called mercy mission?"

"I'm sure we can find someone who will take care of the cats and Dottie. That shouldn't be the most important consideration."

"Easy for you to say, Karen, since the only 'pets' you have are your ceramic chickens. This has been a lot to think about. I need a bit more time before voting," Lynn said as she got up to leave. "I'll let you know this afternoon."

She paused and grinned, "Anyone bringing guacamole?" With that flip comment, Lynn made her exit, leaving Karen and Susan shaking their heads.

"That girl is certainly good with the exits! At least she didn't fart her way out the door."

"I think her training as a nurse is causing her trouble. She's spent a career saving peoples' lives not ending them. I guess I can understand that. We might be doing this without her, even if she decides to come to Mexico with us."

"Do we need a unanimous decision on this one?" Karen asked.

"If Lynn isn't in full agreement, she might be a problem. She can be a loose cannon and, as we all know, she can't keep a secret to save her soul," Susan said. "I wouldn't want her to blab that we helped Margaret kill herself. If she's involved, she'll be less likely to blab."

"I'm slightly encouraged by the guacamole comment.

She's so food obsessed that the allure of all that delicious Mexican food might influence her decision, at least to come with us. When we're in Mexico and living together, Lynn will see Margaret's day to day suffering. Maybe that will change her mind."

"We need to convince her, at least to join us on the trip. Maybe it's time for a little chat with Margaret and Tom. They might be able to talk her into it."

Susan got out her cell phone and made the calls.

CHAPTER 33

The Elephant in the Room

At five sharp the Dames, including Dottie, and Tom gathered at Margaret's for Unhappy Hour. Each brought a Mexican themed appetizer: salsa and chips, *guacamole, chile con queso* dip and tortillas. All the Dames were at least on the same food page. Dottie and booze should lighten the mood.

Tom, wearing a sombrero, welcomed them and offered them their first of many margaritas. Because he was certain they would have a few, he made them very light on the booze. Fire blazing, the Dames and Tom settled in for an evening of discussion.

Margaret had her computer out with the beach front villa website cued up for all to see and it was beautiful. Situated on the beach with a large pool, front and back patios, an outdoor kitchen and a quaint thatched roof palapa looking out to the ocean, the villa had five en suite bedrooms, a large open kitchen, dining and living area—all on one level and all handicap accessible. The villa came with a cook/ housekeeper and gardener. Their hours were flexible, based on their guests' needs. And the best part: a fully stocked kitchen and bar. Margaret, with Tom's help, had arranged for everything, including the necessary medical supplies.

"Holy guacamole, that's a beautiful villa," Lynn said as she got comfortable on Margaret's sectional with the computer on her lap and Dottie looking longingly at Lynn's plate of food. "I've never been to Mexico and I absolutely adore good Mexican food, but I don't know if I could leave my kitties for such a long time," Lynn said in between mouthfuls. Both Susan and Karen smiled, knowing that Margaret had anticipated Lynn's concern.

"I've thought about you and Susan with your animals. I've arranged for three possible house/pet sitters, who come highly recommended I might add, for you to interview. As I see it, we could get by with one, but if you each want someone to spend full time with your pets, I would be okay with that. I've also talked to housekeeping here and all of your apartments will be thoroughly cleaned prior to your return."

"This is costing you a fortune," Lynn said.

"Just consider this your inheritance," Margaret said, laughing. "To Mexico," Margaret said, raising her glass for a toast.

"To Mexico." They all raised their glasses. Dottie barked just once like she understood the toast.

The rest of the evening was passed with no acknowledgment of the trip's real purpose. For that evening they focused on companionship and love for each other, reminiscing about their lives and the adventures they had shared, omitting, of course, their "delicate" hobby. For that evening, at least, the Elephant was ignored.

CHAPTER 34

Almost Shangri-La

One month later

After a comfortable flight in first class with a few glasses of champagne under their belts (Margaret abstaining because of her meds), the Dames and Tom arrived in Cancun Mexico where a handicap accessible luxury van awaited their arrival.

"Holy shit, is that a Mercedes?" Lynn said as she exited the airport, pushing Margaret's wheelchair. Tom was loaded down with luggage.

From the air-conditioned airport, they stepped into temps in the high seventies with low humidity. In other words, they'd entered a Minnesotan's idea of heaven.

"It's summer!" Susan yelled, holding her pale arms up to the sun. "We've finally escaped."

The past winter had been exceptionally brutal with its cold and damp conditions that continued into early April. Minnesotans were not shocked to see snow in April or even May, so they embraced Mexican temps with gusto, bordering on ecstasy.

"This is definitely the time of year to visit Mexico. Warm but not overly hot, low humidity so that my hair doesn't go completely flat, but the best is we've avoided the college and high school kids celebrating Spring Break. I made the mistake of going to Cozumel in March many years ago and all I remember is drunk kids celebrating," Karen said.

"Now it's the old folks' turn," Margaret said, laughing and patting her short curls. The Dames had persuaded her to leave her wigs at home.

"Is that our cutie pie holding a sign that says 'Margaret'?" Karen said.

"We can only hope," Lynn said as she smoothed her wrinkled linen dress and waved to the cutie. "Why is it that your linen doesn't wrinkle and mine does?" Lynn said as she pushed Margaret to the limo. "What is that beautiful hot pink flower over there?" Lynn pointed to a riotous display of hibiscus.

"I was wondering when your ADD would kick in?" Karen said, laughing.

"My linen doesn't wrinkle because I am special and because it's a linen polyester blend," Margaret said.

"You certainly are special," Lynn agreed. Then Lynn looked carefully at her pale and fragile friend. *We're here to help our best friend kill herself. I still don't know if I can. It's good that I'm wearing sun glasses.* Lynn brushed her cheeks.

"Lynn, are you okay?" Margaret asked, jolting Lynn back to the present.

"I'm not used to the sun's brightness; it makes my eyes water. You'll have to tell me where you got that outfit."

"I don't remember where I got the pants—maybe one of those clothes-for-traveling catalogs. I think the flower you noticed is a hibiscus. Or is it an hibiscus."

"You're absolutely right about the flower. I think I left my brain at home."

"That's the beauty of Mexico," Tom said as he joined them. "You can leave your brain at home and still have a wonderful time. The luggage is loaded. Ladies, your carriage awaits."

The cutie, whose name was Francisco, then helped the two women with their wheelchairs into a van equipped with an exceptional sound system, a wet bar with a bottle of champagne on ice, and a flat-screened TV. With a considerable amount of elderly noise, everyone settled in comfortably.

"Oh, goody more champagne," Lynn said with a girlish giggle.

"What did I say earlier about drunk kids celebrating?" Lynn stuck out her tongue at Karen, thus proving Karen's point. Lynn, Karen, Susan, and Tom sipped their wine and looked out at the surrounding beauty.

"I can't believe the expanse of green, the palm trees, the beautiful flowers and we haven't even left the airport," Karen said.

The hour long drive to Puerto went by rapidly with music playing and cheerful conversation. The women were like little kids with their noses pressed against the windows, all except Margaret who was resting, holding hands with Tom.

"You've got the travel brochure, Susan. Tell us what they say about Puerto," Tom said as they neared their destination.

Susan opened the brochure and started to read:

> *Puerto Aventuras is a community located in Solidaridad Municipality, Quintana Roo, Mexico. It had a 2010 census population of 5,979 inhabitants, and is located at an elevation of nine metres (Thirty feet) above sea level. It is the second-largest community in Solidaridad Municipality, after the municipal seat, Playa del Carmen.*
>
> *Puerto Aventuras is divided into two parts: west of Highway 307 is the residential subdivision, east of Highway 307 along the Caribbean coast is the tourist zone with hotels and resorts, part of the Riviera Maya.*

"Stop. You're putting me to sleep," Lynn said.

"The three or four glasses of champagne might have something to do with it," Karen commented.

"Blah, blah, blah," Lynn countered.

"I don't know about the rest of you, but I'm ready for a nap," Tom said as they exited for Puerto Aventuras.

"Me too," Karen agreed.

"Any info about restaurants and fun stuff to do? That's what I'm interested in, not boring details about elevation and population." Lynn yawned.

"How about we save the fun stuff for after our naps?" Everyone agreed to a nap until ... they saw *The Villa*.

Lynn led the group in a chorus of "Holy shits."

The Mercedes limo pulled into the driveway of Casa del Mar, a contemporary pale yellow stucco villa that overlooked the Caribbean. With the sun backlighting the villa and the red hibiscus, yellow lantana and hot pink bougainvillea dancing in the breeze, palm trees lining the driveway, the Dames were convinced they'd entered another world. Mouths open, the Dames stared at their temporary home.

"Well, ladies, what do you think?" They were speechless, an unusual occurrence for these women. "The website certainly didn't do it justice," Margaret said.

A large stone patio with huge ceramic pots of exotic blooms lined each side of the walkway.

"Talk about curb appeal," Lynn said, the first to regain speech. "I wonder if I could grow some of these at home."

Susan stopped wheeling to examine an exotic bloom. The others ignored the plants, eager to examine the villa's opulent interior.

The house was designed to display the optimum ocean view, so from the minute a visitor walked through the front door she could see the pool, the outdoor patio surrounding it and the white sands of the Caribbean.

They were greeted by a beautiful young woman standing in the doorway.

"Welcome to Casa del Mar. My name is Maria and I will be your cook and housekeeper for the month." She smiled warmly.

"Phillip will bring in your luggage and take it to your rooms. Just follow him. When you're settled and refreshed, in say an hour, let's meet back here in the main living area for some modest refreshments. Feel free to wander about in the meantime. I'll be in the kitchen if you have any questions." She was dressed casually in a loose-fitting aqua and yellow flowered shift, colors that were echoed in the interior.

Lynn whispered, "She's color coordinated with the house. Can you believe it?" Karen just smiled, still speechless.

"Hurry up. The Wheelies are gaining on us."

"This is amazing, a Shangri-La, a paradise, a dream come true," Karen paused.

"Except for Margaret."

Karen finally found her voice.

CHAPTER 35

Butts, Bees 'n' Bonnets

"Does my bathing suit make my butt look big?" Lynn said as she walked slowly down the steps and into the swimming pool. Lynn was wearing a hot pink and yellow print one piece with a ruffly skirt which amplified her ample derriere.

"Would you care if it did?" Karen asked, laughing. "Everything makes your butt look big. Personally I've embraced my flab and my crepey skin. I think it's time you did as well." Karen was kicking her feet in the water, occasionally splashing her pal. "You look good for an old lady."

"I'm in my happy place, so you can't goad me into an argument and you're right I do have a big butt, but I'm sure I read someplace that as you get older, it's a good idea to carry some extra weight. You know, in case of an emergency."

"Then we both should be good in an emergency."

Susan rolled onto the patio to join in the fun. She was wearing a tasteful black tankini.

"You look fabulous, girlfriend," Karen said. "How do you like your room?"

"It's gorgeous. Plus it's totally set up for someone in a wheelchair. I will be able to shower and get dressed, without help just like at home. Margaret has thought of everything. Now if I could only figure out how to get in the pool."

Just then Phillip emerged from the kitchen. "Would you like help getting into the water, *Senora?* We often rent to people with special needs and I've become quite good at helping them. I would suggest a floatation device."

"I would love to, Phillip, if you don't mind." Minutes later Senorita Susan was floating around the pool relaxed and happy.

"I'll be in the kitchen helping Maria with your evening meal if you need anything," Philipp said with a smile.

"I think I'm in love," Lynn said as she dried herself off.

"With Phillip or the Casa?"

"Yes. Is this heaven or what?" Lynn said, looking at the gardens surrounding the pool. "I wonder if I could take some cuttings home."

"Not going to happen. It's against the rules: no plants allowed," Karen said.

"Party pooper."

"When you two are done squabbling, I think we need to check in with Margaret."

"Si, Senora."

The Dames went to Margaret's suite to thank her once again for her generosity. They were shocked when they discovered the hospital bed, the IV equipment and the commode, but being good friends, they kept their thoughts to themselves.

An hour later the Dames, without Margaret, were showered and dressed for what looked to be a fabulous dinner of freshly caught sea bass, salad, and seasoned rice. Maria had set the table on the patio with candles, and a fire was blazing in the outdoor fireplace. After that fine meal, they adjourned to the lounge chairs placed around the fire. The stars were bright, the air was cooling, the pool glistened in the moonlight.

"Now that was a perfect ending to a perfect day. I'm exhausted," Lynn said as she lazily sipped the last of her wine. They were all feeling relaxed and mellow except for Tom who seemed a bit restless.

"I should be getting back to Margaret."

"Before you go, I'd like to know how Margaret is—really," Susan asked Tom. "We were shocked to see all the hospital equipment."

"I'm sad to say not good at all." Tom paused to gain control over his emotions.

"She was a real trooper today. The travel must have been hard on her," Susan said. "I felt it and I don't have stage four cancer. She must have been hurting."

"Margaret doesn't complain even when she's in great discomfort. She tends to minimize her pain even though it is increasing daily. The pain has gone from being localized to being generalized. In other words, she hurts all over her body."

"Is there any chance at all that she will improve?"

"I would like to be able to say yes, but her condition will only worsen. I can keep her comfortable with powerful narcotics, but that's the best I can do. It's important she receive these drugs on a regular schedule. With today's excitement and travel, she missed one of her pills and suffered as a result. But she ate a bit of soup and pudding, took her pill and is resting comfortably. Eventually I'll have to insert an IV to administer the medication. Hopefully a good night's sleep will perk her up. She wants to spend as much time with you as possible."

"Will she be able to go on some field trips with us like to *Talum* or *Chichen Itza?*"

"Probably not, but she will be able to go on some walks in the village, nothing too long or strenuous. I'll stay with her while you ladies have some adventures. She wouldn't want to slow you down."

"I don't know how to ask this... " Karen said.

"You want to know when, right?"

"Right."

"I can't really tell you. Margaret will know when it's time, but I believe it will be sooner rather than later." Tom's voice cracked. "Excuse me. I need a walk. Good night, ladies."

The Dames were silent for some time.

Maria broke the silence to say goodnight.

"Maria, the meal was excellent. Thanks so much for everything."

"I'm sorry about your friend. I'll help however I can."

"We know."

"Excuse me, ladies, I have an important phone call to make," Susan said without explanation.

"Who put a bee in her bonnet?"

"It's called Love."

CHAPTER 36

Sting, Stang, Stung

The Dames sans Margaret spent the next three days exploring Maya Riviera: the ruins in *Coba, Tulum,* and *Chichen Itza* while Margaret and Tom spent quiet days sitting around the pool and taking occasional "walks" to the village. Margaret was weakening by the day.

On their fourth day in Paradise, Lynn and Karen decided to try snorkeling. With Phillip's advice and instruction, the Dames waddled out to the pool wearing flippers, masks, and sporting zinc-covered noses. Phillip stressed the need for getting used to breathing with the mouthpieces before going in the ocean. A good piece of advice, considering they were totally unfamiliar with the equipment and the ocean.

"Shit, how are you supposed to move in these flippers," Lynn said as she banged into a chaise lounge.

"I can't see a damn thing," Karen said.

"You're supposed to wait until you get to the water before putting the mask on."

"Right." Karen took off her mask.

"There's nothing to see once we get in the pool anyway. I want to see the pretty blue and yellow parrot fish that I've seen on those *Nature* shows. I say we try the ocean instead of the pool."

"Probably not a good idea until we get the hang of breathing with this tube thingy and walking with these flippers. Now I know how seals feel," Karen said.

Once they got to the pool, they jumped in and floated on their bellies breathing through the mouthpiece and tube, unfortunately taking in water.

"I think I just swallowed half the pool," Lynn said, coughing and spitting.

"Just be glad it's not salt water or you'd be one sick puppy," Karen said.

From their room, Margaret and Tom watched their friends' comical attempts. "It's Ethel and Lucy trying to snorkel," Tom said, laughing.

"I especially like the white zinc stripe on their noses. God, I'm going to miss them."

After a few laps studying the tiled pool bottom, the Dames got bored and decided to try the "real" thing.

"Let's ditch these flippers if we're just going to wade in shallow water," Karen said.

So they walked to the beach barefoot, waded to thigh height and started to swim, faces in the water. After a few more accidental swigs and spits of disgusting salt water, the Dames decided to abandon their breathing "tube thingys" and just look at the pretty fish swimming in the clear water. That's when Lynn spotted the stingray spread out on the sandy bottom.

"Karen, look at the stingray. Isn't it beautiful?"

"Where?"

"Right where ... "

Karen let out an impressive shriek.

"Looks like you found it."

Margaret and Tom heard Karen's scream. "Stay here, Margaret. I'll get Phillip."

Lynn helped Karen to shore and then proceeded to do the most unusual thing: she squatted over Karen's foot and peed.

"What the hell are you doing? I'm in pain and you're taking a leak?"

"I'm trying to help ease the pain just like in that *Friends* episode when Monica gets stung by a stingray and Joey, or was it Chandler, peed on her foot."

"That was a jelly fish and it was Chandler who peed."

"Whatever."

"My foot really hurts and your pee didn't help at all."

"That's because I missed and I think I'm running on empty. Anyway it's the thought that counts."

By this time Phillip and Tom had run down to the beach. Lynn explained as best she could what happened while Karen moaned in pain.

Phillip sighed and said, "Now do you understand why I didn't want you out in the ocean? We've had some problems with stingrays before. Fortunately, I know what to do. Plus we have a doctor on the scene. You're a lucky lady." Karen growled her response.

"Come on, let's get you inside."

Tom and Phillip administered first aid by soaking Karen's foot in very hot water to dissipate the venom. Then with a tweezers, Tom removed the barb, dabbed antibiotic cream on the wound, and then loosely bandaged Karen's foot which was beginning to swell. He then gave her an antibiotic and a pain pill and handed Lynn several more pain pills to be administered six hours apart. Tom and Phillip assured her that the sting wasn't fatal. "You'll just be uncomfortable for a few days."

Karen was about to complain when she looked at Margaret in her wheelchair and felt ashamed.

"Thanks for everything. I'd like to go to my room now."

"Guess I can cross that off my bucket list," Karen said as Lynn helped her get comfortable in bed.

"You had a stingray bite on your bucket list?"

"No, you dumb shit, I had snorkeling on my bucket list."

"Maybe you should change to a fuck-it list," Lynn said, laughing at her joke.

"Mock me, if you will, but this really hurts and I never even got a good look at the stingray." Karen yawned. "I think the pain pill Tom gave me is starting to work. Everyone should travel with their own personal physician and their own stash of drugs. Phillip was right. I am a lucky lady." Another huge yawn.

"Apparently stings happen." What Lynn really meant was, "Stop whining. I'd like to move on to a more pleasant topic." And she did.

"Have I told you about the concert my daughter and I went to at the X-cell center? Sting and Paul Simon. He sang like an angel and looked devilishly handsome. Funny thing, Paul Simon's band lost all power half way through the show, and Sting had to sing 'Bridge Over Troubled Waters' *a capella.* Beautiful, just beautiful. You know, don't you, about tantric sex? He's famous for it." Lynn sighed and looked over at her good friend who was snoring peacefully.

Patting her sleeping friend's hand, she whispered "Good night, dear friend" and went back to her room, took out her computer and looked up tantric sex, having no clue what it was.

CHAPTER 37

Chill Pill Anyone?

"We look like casualties of war," Karen said as she hobbled into the dining room with the crutches Phillip had found in the storage shed. "Two in wheelchairs and one on crutches. Lynn and Tom, you're the only ones still ambulatory. Let's see what we can do about that," Karen said as she playfully swiped at Lynn and gently poked Tom in the tummy with her crutch.

"Someone is feeling much better," Susan said.

"Sixteen hours of sleep and two pain pills help."

"I say better living through drugs," Lynn said with a grin.

Margaret, Susan, Tom and Lynn were sitting around the table eating a lovely breakfast of fresh fruit and yogurt. A basket of pastries from the local bakery, pots of coffee and tea sat on the contemporary sideboard. Margaret picked at her food while the others, especially Lynn, seemed ravenous.

The doors to the patio were open and the sun was shining. Just another day in Paradise.

In the middle of breakfast and amiable conversation, Susan excused herself and wheeled out to the patio, leaving her friends shaking their heads.

"What's up with her? That was an abrupt departure."

"My, she seems fidgety these last few days," Margaret said.

"No, I'd say agitated is more like it," Tom said.

"Well, I say we take the 'bull by the horns' and ask her." Lynn, known for her bluntness, went out to the patio to confront Susan who was staring at the ocean.

"What's going on, Susan? You seem like a dog in a room filled with fire hydrants or maybe a 'cat on a hot tin roof.' That's better."

"I kind of like the dog simile myself... So you noticed."

"We all noticed."

"Well, I guess now's as good a time as any since you'll all know by this afternoon anyhow. Let's do it." And she rolled back into the house to enlighten her concerned friends.

"Seems you've all been baffled by my behavior. I haven't been myself these last few days because I've been sitting on a secret. So here goes." Susan took a big breath and let her happiness explode. "Steve will be arriving in Cozumel late this afternoon and we plan to be married right here on the beach."

The Dames gasped and then blasted Susan with questions. "When?"

"Will you stay here for your honeymoon?"

"Seriously?"

"Can we see your dress?"

"Is it legal?"

"Who's going to officiate?"

"Who will be your maid of honor?"

"Whoa, one at a time. We have to take care of getting the license and all that bureaucratic nonsense. According to my research, that takes three or four days, so I guess in three or four days. Yes, it will be legal. I don't have a dress and we need to find a justice of the peace or whatever they call them here. Oh, and yes, I'm ... we're serious."

"You forgot the honeymoon question," Karen reminded her.

"And the maid of honor question." Lynn fluttered her eyelashes as if to say *"moi."*

Susan paused for a few seconds and looked at Margaret. "Margaret, would you be my Best Woman?"

"What about the honeymoon?"

"And is it okay for us to stay here for our honeymoon?"

Margaret started to cry and simply nodded her head. Tom reached over to take her hand in his. At this tender gesture all the Dames started to cry. As they looked at each other crying away, Lynn started to laugh and soon everyone was joining her. Tom looked overwhelmed and somewhat confused by the sudden switch of emotions.

Margaret was the first to gain control. "We have some planning to do, don't we girls? But first we need to celebrate with mimosas. I think we have a few bottles of bubbly in the fridge. Lynn, would you please ask Maria?"

"What's all the noise about?" Maria asked when she walked into the dining room with the champagne and freshly squeezed orange juice. She looked at the smiles filling the dining room and immediately understood. "Oh, I see. You finally told them."

"You mean Maria knew before the rest of us?" Karen asked, looking at Maria. "You're good, girl. I wouldn't want to play poker with you!" The Dames laughed at the reference to their many evenings of poker.

"Well, I didn't want to spring it on her because of the extra preparations—food, flowers, you know, so yes, I told her first."

"No apologies needed," Margaret said. "We're thrilled with the news. When will Steve arrive?"

"He lands in Cozumel at four-thirty. After the ferry ride to Playa, Phillip will pick him up and with luck he'll be here around seven or so."

Maria and Phillip served the mimosas.

"Orange juice only for Karen and Margaret," Tom insisted.

"Party pooper," Karen said.

"Congratulations to the happy couple!" Margaret held up her glass. "To Love!"

"To Love!"

"I've always wanted to be a wedding planner." Lynn giggled as she drank her bubbly.

"I'm so glad I'm wounded," Karen whispered to Lynn. "I hate weddings."

"Suck it up. Too bad you can't have anything to drink. Take a pill and chill," Lynn said as she gave Karen her pain pill. "Doctor's orders."

CHAPTER 38

Shop 'Til You Drop

"I don't want a foo-foo wedding dress. I think my cream colored pant suit is just fine."

"A pant suit? You've got to be kidding me. A bride should wear a beautiful dress."

"So says the woman with three divorces."

"I'm going to forget you said that, Lynn." Karen gimped to the rack with more formal dresses. "This would look wonderful on you." Karen held up a pink silk long dress."

"I hate pink, I don't wear dresses, and this looks like a slip or a nightgown."

"Sexy, though," Lynn said. She wandered off to find something for herself and disappeared into the dressing room with her arms full.

"A Bridzilla moment," Lynn mumbled to herself from the dressing room where she was trying on various inappropriate sundresses.

"Nothing fits right," she said, modeling a bright yellow halter top sundress, her ample chest oozing out the front and the back. "It must be the sizing here in Mexico."

"Just face it: You're terminally chubby and elderly. Besides yellow is not your color."

Tom was sitting in an overstuffed chair with a glass of wine, wishing he had the entire bottle. Steve, lucky man that he was, was avoiding the wedding preparations by doing some sightseeing on his own.

"How about this?" Margaret said as she held up an embroidered white on white cotton flared long sleeve over-blouse with a pair of pants to match. "It's white and the blouse is hand-made. Look at the intricate embroidery, the tiny stitches, the beautiful design. You'd be wearing a work of art. Plus it's practical enough that you could actually wear it again."

"Long sleeves?"

"It gets chilly after the sun goes down. Simple, beautiful, it's perfect. You know me well and that's why you're my Best Woman," Susan said as she and Margaret held hands. "I'll pay for this and we can go home. You're looking tired, Margaret."

"You know me well," Margaret said.

"And what are we? Chopped liver?"

"You're my Best Girls."

"It's better than nothing. At least we don't have to wear ugly bridesmaids' dresses."

"What are we going to wear, by the way?" Karen said to Lynn as they left the boutique.

"I'm sure you will look lovely whatever you decide," Margaret said, her voice barely audible.

"We need to get this Best Woman home. She's had enough for today," Tom said.

"What about the flowers?" Lynn said.

"I'll let you three figure that out," Margaret said.

"Phillip will come back to pick you up after he drops us off. Just stay put." Tom wheeled Margaret to the van.

"She really doesn't look good at all," Susan said. "If she can just hold on until tomorrow... "

"I'm surprised she's made it this long; your wedding has given her a reason to live. We've had some wonderful times these last few days. Beautiful memories."

'Speaking of beautiful memories... we forgot about a photographer! I doubt we can get one on such short notice."

"Relax, Karen. Phillip, our very own Renaissance man,

has promised to take pictures. Maria says he's very good."

"Music—you want music don't you?"

"Chill, girlfriend. I brought along my Bill Evans CDs. Maria is catering. It's all under control. We only have Margaret to worry about. Now let's go buy us some flowers," Susan said, as Phillip pulled up the Mercedes.

CHAPTER 39

An Almost Perfect Day

Casa del Mar was a flurry of activity the day of the wedding. Even though there would be very few guests, preparations were elaborate. Maria had been baking for days; she had her family help with the cleaning and gardening while she continued preparations for a traditional Mexican wedding feast. Each guest would get a copy of the menu:

APPETIZERS:
Seafood in Puff Pastry and
Pheasant Consommé with Morels
served with Sauvignon blanc

FIRST COURSE:
White Fish with Sesame Seeds and Cascabel Peppers
served with Chardonnay

MAIN COURSE:
Lobster-Stuffed Filet Mignon with Two Moles
served with Merlot

DESSERTS:
Goat Cheese Cheesecake with Quince Jelly,
Coconut Tequila Sorbet
Sonoran Cream Cake with White Chocolate Leaves

Mexican Coffee and Mexican Sweets
served with champagne

The flowers arrived in the early afternoon and were quickly placed inside where the cooler temps would keep them from wilting. Maria and Phillip would place them outside before the 7:00 p.m. ceremony.

"What are 'Two Moles' anyway?" Lynn asked when she saw the menu. "Aren't those the little rodents that wreck lawns?"

"Could be a great name for a band."

"If we had one glass of every wine mentioned in the menu, we'd be soused by the end of the meal."

"Sounds like your kind of wedding," Karen said, laughing. "Let's check with Maria about the moles and ask if she needs help."

Maria took a few minutes to explain about moles: "I like to make a 'sour fruit' variety using tomatillos and a sweet variety using raisins and other dried fruit. I first roast and then dry chili peppers. Once they're dried, I grind them up with spices such as cinnamon, cloves and cumin. Finally, I add the fruit and water and simmer until fairly thick. Sometimes I add almonds and chocolate as thickeners. We're having one with tomatillos and one with raisins. I hope you like them."

"And what are cascabel peppers?"

"We grow them in pots on the front patio. I must warn you: They're very hot so don't eat one whole. I will dice a small amount for flavoring the white fish which is normally quite bland, but I mainly use them for a pretty garnish. They come with a warning! I'll be sure to make a small amount of white fish for Margaret; I know she prefers bland food. Anything else?"

"Can we help with anything?" Karen asked.

"No, I think I'm okay for the moment. Thanks for offering."

"My work here is done," Lynn said.

"No, honey, your work is just beginning: hair, nails, makeup."

"First things first: a siesta."

"Right on, girlfriend."

Karen and Lynn went to their rooms to prepare for the ceremony, which for them included naps followed by frenzied attempts to remove the sleep wrinkles and repair damaged hair-dos. Margaret and Tom were sequestered in their bedroom while Susan was doing what brides do on their big day: fussing. The groom-to-be hadn't been seen since breakfast.

The wedding party emerged from their respective lairs a half hour before the ceremony. The men, dressed casually in white and tan linen, went directly to the back patio for a glass of bubbly, while the women planned their grand entrances. Karen, dressed tastefully in black slacks and a black silk blouse commensurate with her hatred of weddings, hobbled in first; Lynn, wearing a turquoise and cream print long dress, followed, pushing Margaret, lovely and delicate as always, in her shell pink linen pant suit. Susan, holding a bouquet of white and yellow calla lilies and wearing her new artistic, handmade blouse and pants, was last. Phillip had asked if he could walk her down the aisle and she gratefully accepted. If she had been back in Minnesota, Dottie would have walked her down the aisle. Bill Evans and his *Plays for Lovers* album accompanied the procession.

The setting sun over the Carribean, the cozy fire, the candles, the flowers, the music, all added to the romance.

Then there was the officiant, swarthy, short, and sturdy, who spoke in Spanish. For all Susan and Steve knew they had promised to love, honor, and rob a bank in Playa. The good news: The service was short and apparently legal. Just as the officiant supposedly said in Spanish, "You may kiss the bride," or "You may squat on a cactus," the *Mariachi* band, consisting of Maria's cousin, uncle, and brother, arrived and the party began with a bang—literally. Maria had arranged for a small display of fireworks on the beach. Another cousin, this one with a penchant for explosives.

"Thank God that went off without a hitch. I was worried when no one had seen Steve all day. His track record for weddings isn't the best," Karen said. Now that she was off the pain meds, she sipped a glass of bubbly with her feet up on the chaise lounge. "See, my foot doesn't look too disgusting, does it?" She shoved her bruised and swollen foot in Lynn's face.

"Jeez Louise, I don't want to see or smell your sting-ray damaged foot," Lynn said.

"Besides I'm starving and ready for some of that fancy schmancy Mexican wedding food. Bring on the 'two moles.'"

"Dinner is served."

"Talk about perfect timing."

Lynn helped Karen up from her chair and the BFFs seated themselves at the long, beautifully decorated table. Instead of a large centerpiece bouquet, Susan opted for a series of small, colorful arrangements, one for each of the guests to take to their rooms.

Phillip and Maria served the food; the guests devoured the culinary delights and drank more wine than they should have. This continued until the last course was served.

Tipsy and delightfully happy, the guests ended the evening with a toast from Tom:

"To a beautiful couple on a perfect night ... be happy, laugh and love with abandon."

"If you'll allow me to follow with a toast of my own." Susan looked at Margaret. "And to Margaret's generosity and continued love and support ... we cherish your friendship. Just know you are loved." Susan lifted her glass.

"Hear, hear," and everyone lifted a final glass in honor of Susan, Steve, and Margaret, their dearest friend.

"There I go blubbering again," Lynn said as she wiped her eyes.

"You're not the only one," Karen said, glancing at Phillip and Maria.

"I'm going to take Margaret to her room. It's been a lovely day and a wonderful party. Thanks so much for including me in all the festivities. Maybe I'll join you later."

"It's been a perfect day, hasn't it? I'm ready to go," Margaret whispered to Tom as he wheeled her to their room.

Four hours later Margaret was gone.

CHAPTER 40

"I Am Going Home."

Margaret and Tom had arranged for a mortuary in Playa to pick up her remains for cremation. She insisted on making her trip home as simple as possible. She also insisted that Steve and Susan stay the remainder of the month for their honeymoon.

Lynn and Karen decided to accompany Tom on the flight back to Minnesota. Without Margaret, they didn't have the heart to stay in Mexico, nor did they want to intrude on the newlyweds.

About an hour into the flight, Tom opened his brief case and handed Karen a large sealed envelope. "I haven't looked at this yet because I haven't had the emotional strength or the energy. It contains Margaret's plans for the service and reception. All I want to do now is sleep." He turned on the light for the flight attendant. Shortly thereafter she brought him a blanket and a pillow.

"Can I get you ladies anything?" They both ordered white wine.

"Isn't flying first class amazing?" Lynn looked in Tom's direction, but he was sound asleep.

"Poor guy. He must be exhausted. These last few weeks have been so difficult for him and for all of us; talk about being on call twenty-four / seven . That's what I call really amazing," Karen said.

"He certainly went above and beyond, that's for sure." Lynn paused to take a drink and stared at the envelope in Karen's hand like it was a dangerous insect about to bite.

"Who keeps a death envelope anyway? It's just plain weird and sort of creepy."

"Weird maybe, but not creepy. Actually it's a very Margaret thing to do when I think about it. Look how she organized her life: her closets with the dresses, pants and blouses sorted by color with uniform hangers all hanging in the same direction. I mean she alphabetized her spices. She needed to be in control at all times and she was, for the most part."

"Except for getting the big C—no control there."

"There is that. She exercised, ate right, kept her stress down. She did everything right, yet still got sick. Guess we're all trees in a potential storm." Karen took another sip. "I still think having a plan makes sense. I might investigate a bit when I get home."

"I saw an article in a magazine somewhere, maybe the doctor's office or it could have been at the dentist's. Your tree comment reminded me."

"And your point is?"

"Do you want to be cremated?"

"ADD alert. I think so. I should talk to the kids about it. Can you get back to your story?"

"Right. Well, you can buy this kit, I don't know what else to call it, that provides you with fertilizer, compost, good dirt and a sapling of your choice. You, well not you, 'cause you're dead, but someone mixes your ashes with the dirt and stuff. Plant the sapling and *voila*! You become a tree! I like the idea of being recycled into a tree. What kind of tree would you like to be?"

"Seriously?"

"Okay, you're not in the mood for small talk. I get it. So open the damn envelope; I'm curious as hell."

"Don't get your undies in a bundle," Karen said as she followed Lynn's instructions.

"Read them aloud."

Karen unfolded a hand-written letter written on Margaret's expensive stationery addressed to all of them:

> *My Dear Friends,*
>
> *If you are reading this, you are beginning to prepare for my service and reception. With Tom's help, I have tried to make this as easy for you as possible. Since he is my executor, he will take care of the finances.*
>
> *Now, for the service... I've always loved Dvorak's New World Symphony...*

The letter went on to detail additional music, readings, flowers, food, and beverages. She ended the letter with a very personal message to the Dames:

> *I'd like each of you to take anything you admire from the apartment, something to remember me by. I also have some lovely jewelry that I've amassed over the years, thanks to the husbands. It would give me great pleasure to see you wearing some of my "sparklies." Bling becomes you.*
>
> *Don't be shy, Lynn, I know you want the male nude painting in my bedroom. And Tiff has admired the abstract painting above the fireplace. She said it was Kandinsky meets Cezanne, a brilliant insight actually. She deserves to own it.*
>
> *I've given the apartment and whatever you don't want to Tom, my darling sweet man, and set up a college/apartment fund for Tiffany. I've asked Tom to sell the Mustang and donate the money to breast cancer research. That pretty much takes care of my assets.*

I want to thank you for the support, the encouragement, the love and the laughter.

You've made me laugh when I didn't think I could ever laugh again. And the adventures we've shared along the way ... I've loved every one and I've loved you. I am so grateful for our friendship. Men come and men go (all except Steve and Tom), but women friends last a lifetime.

Remember: "Always look on the bright side of life."

Until we meet again ...

Love,

   Margaret

P.S. Susan, give Dottie a treat and a cuddle for me.

CHAPTER 41

Blings and Things

Six weeks later

> *Get Father Patrick to officiate.*

Check.

> *Invite all of the community to the service.*

Check.

> *Tell them to take the flowers, booze and left-over food.*

Check.

> *Take what you want from the apartment.*

Check.

> *Give the rest away.*

Check

> *Give the painting to Tiff.*

Check.

> *etc... etc ... etc ...*

> *Sprinkle my ashes in the perennial garden.*

They had boxed and donated Margaret's clothes, cleaned out the pantry and given the food to food shelves, taken what household cleaning supplies they could use, and thrown out partially used beauty products. The Dames took some towels and bedding for themselves and donated the rest. Tom wanted the bedroom suite, the patio furniture, and some of the living and dining room furniture.

The Dames went over Margaret's detailed instructions several times to make sure everything was in place. In the past few weeks they had worked their booties off, crossing almost everything off their lengthy "to do" list. Only one thing remained.

Once they got over the feeling they were robbing their dear friend, the Dames enjoyed "shopping" in Margaret's apartment.

Karen took the few "antiques": a hand-carved German clock that was in Margaret's guest room and a vintage hand-pieced quilt made by Margaret's grandmother. She also wanted the diamond filigree Victorian brooch and a pair of diamond studs.

Susan took several hand-blown glass vases, the pottery pieces, and the watercolor from Margaret's last husband, a gift commemorating their honeymoon. Having recently returned from her honeymoon, it was a fitting choice. She also succumbed to the allure of a simple emerald and gold ring.

Then there was Lynn who wandered around in total confusion, from one room to another like a kid spending her piggy bank savings, taking hours to make a decision. She would pick up a beautiful vase and then run to the jewelry box to try on some bling. She finally ended up with Margaret's leather recliner, her flat screened TV, and a framed and signed photograph of an Italian harbor because she spied a cat hiding on one of the boats.

"Don't you want a piece of jewelry?" Karen asked.

"Oh, I don't know. I'm feeling a bit guilty at the moment. Like maybe I'm taking too much."

"She specifically instructed us to take a piece or two of jewelry. And Margaret must be obeyed," Susan said, chuckling.

"Oh, all right." Lynn walked over to the jewelry box and tried on several necklaces and bracelets. "What do you think? The pearl necklace with the diamond clasp or the ruby and diamond tennis bracelet?"

Susan wheeled over to Lynn, dangling a velvet jewelry bag in front of her. Along with the jewelry was a note from Margaret:

> Lynn, this was to be your Christmas gift. I
> found it and I thought of you. Merry Christmas.

It was a diamond and garnet encrusted pin in the shape of a piece of strawberry cheesecake. The Dames burst into laughter.

"How did you know this was in there?" Lynn asked.

"When you were wandering around for the last hour or so, I seriously examined the jewelry and found this. It's perfect."

"It certainly is," Lynn said, holding the pin up to the light.

"Let's celebrate and thank our dear friend for these lovely treasures. I say we open the bottle of bubbly I put in the refrigerator." Karen went into the kitchen to fetch four champagne glasses.

"You got four glasses, Karen."

"Habit, I guess. It's going to take awhile to get used to the fact that she's really gone." Karen poured champagne in all four glasses.

"To Margaret, thank you for these gifts."

"We will cherish them always."

"We will always remember you." The Dames clinked glasses and toasted their dear friend.

When Lynn finished her own glass, she hoisted Margaret's: "She wouldn't want me to waste the bubbly."

"You're too much, girlfriend," Karen said.

"Speaking of 'too much,' would it be too much to wear our jewelry to the service tomorrow? I wouldn't want people to think we were showing off."

"I doubt they'd even notice," Karen said.

"Margaret would be very pleased," Lynn said, pinning her jeweled cheesecake bling to her ample chest, emitting a delicate burp as she did so.

CHAPTER 42

"I have an idea... "

"My, don't you girls look lovely with all your jewels. I don't believe I've seen you wearing so much jewelry before," Mrs. Simonson said after the service. She was carrying her Mary Poppins bag as usual. She continued, "I'm so sorry for your loss. Mrs. Thompson was a real jewel herself."

"Yes, she was. We will miss her terribly," Lynn said as Mrs. Simonson toddled off for more food and another drink.

"I thought you said no one would notice," Lynn whispered to Karen.

"Doesn't matter. No one cares. Let it go, Lynn. We should be very grateful she didn't pull out her 'device' and show us pictures of her grandkids."

"Or offer us spiked tea," Lynn said, laughing. "Where are Susan and Steve anyhow?"

"They're currently surrounded by well-wishers congratulating them on their marriage and welcoming Steve to the community. They're not going to save us."

"And could this day get any better?" Lynn said as they watched Tiffany and Bob Miller approach them. Tiff had been crying.

"Mr. Miller, it's so good to see you out and about. How are you feeling after your accident?"

"A broken hip ain't no fun, I tell ya, girlie. Talk about clumsy—I tripped over a pair of shoes I left in the middle of the room. Edith always told me to put away my shoes. Guess I should a listened."

"How long will you have to use a walker?"

"Yeah, she was a talker, my Edith."

"Bob, she said 'walker,'" Tiff said very loudly.

"Broken hip, hearing gone—getting old ain't for sissies, that's for sure. So sorry about Margaret; she was a classy girlie-girl. Always looked like a million bucks and she could make a mean lemon bar besides."

"Margaret was so good to me and I never had the chance to thank her for her generous help." Tiff broke into tears again. "I can only promise you that I will finish college and try to honor her memory by paying it forward when I can. I've rented a one bedroom apartment across from the Institute of Arts, but will look in on Bob as often as I can. It's my turn to help him. Thank you for everything." They walked to the buffet table.

The reception seemed to go on for hours, but finally the guests began to disperse.

"Don't forget to help yourself to the leftovers and please take some of the flowers." Karen, Lynn, and Susan reminded their friends.

"Look, Mrs. Simonson just took a bouquet of lilies and stuffed them in her bag."

"I'm surprised she has any room, considering she also has a bottle of brandy and plastic containers filled with leftovers. That woman is a hoot!"

"That she is."

"Margaret would have enjoyed her party," Susan said.

"I think she has," Karen said.

"Now, there's only one thing left to do. Let's meet tomorrow morning around ten in the gardens. I'll bring Margaret and the bags," Susan said.

"Maggie in a Baggie," Lynn said, laughing at her own joke.

"Love it!"

* * *

It was a beautiful summer day: sunny, warm, no wind. A perfect day for scattering ashes. Margaret would be pleased.

The Dames, with their Maggie baggies and Dottie, carefully scattered their dear friend's ashes in her beloved perennial gardens, but saved enough for the tree they were planting in her honor. The gardeners had dug the hole and prepared it for planting. The yellow flowering "butterflies magnolia" tree had been delivered and was ready to plant.

"Susan, would you do the honors?" Karen said. Susan simply nodded and poured the remainder of Margaret's ashes into the hole.

"Margaret, we hope you like yellow magnolias. We know you like butterflies and spring. Magnolias are delicate, but strong—like you."

"Godspeed, dear friend."

The Dames wiped their eyes and headed back, leaving the actual planting to the gardeners. They were elderly, after all.

"However will we spend our spare time now that Margaret isn't around to organize game nights?" Karen said.

"I've been thinking about our game nights," Lynn said.

"Ooh, Lynn's thinking. That's dangerous," Susan said.

"I'm ignoring that. I think we're too old for this 'Pop Goes the Weasel' game. I almost hurt myself during Operation Switcheroo. We weren't that good at it anyway. Maybe we should stick with poker," Karen said.

"You're probably right."

"I have an idea." The Dames looked at Lynn and rolled their eyes — again.

"It's always dangerous when you have an idea or think," Susan said.

"Well, I was on the Internet shopping for my granddaughter and I saw this woman who used roadkill squirrels to make dolls." At the mention of squirrels, Dottie's ears perked up and she looked around for the furry rodents.

"Of course, you couldn't use the squashed ones. You wouldn't believe the stuffed squirrel Liberace doll—wearing a cape of sequins and white fake fur, at least I think it was fake, though, I suppose, it could have been albino squirrel fur." At each mention of "squirrel," Dottie became hyper-alert. "Anyway, it's sitting in front of this little white piano. Absolutely adorable ... and only $49.99 plus postage. We could make ourselves tons of money."

Just then a squirrel ran directly in front of Dottie. She stopped, lifted her paw and pointed, like a hunting dog. No pulling, no barking. Absolute stillness. The Dames stopped as well, savoring the silence and the beauty of their surroundings.

"That's amazing! She must have some hunting dog in her—maybe German short-hair," Karen said.

"That's as good a guess as any. Steve thought she might be part Doberman and pit bull. Maybe some Dalmatian in the mix. I could have her DNA tested, but I kind of like imagining her genetics. Lynn, what's your take on Dottie's background?"

"She's really gone isn't she?" Lynn started to cry again.

"Yes, dear, she's really gone." Karen put her arm around Lynn and delicately pulled her closer.

"Come on, let's get you home."

The End

Acknowlegments

Suzan St. Maur: my UK writing buddy, prolific author, blogger, and public speaker with a wicked sense of humor. Scammed by the same bogus agent years ago, Suze and I became fast friends as a result. All in all, one formidable Dame.

Judith Bergerson: my old high school chum and fabulous artist. Cover artist for the *Toby Martin* series, and now *Delicate Dames*. Judy adds some class to my endeavors. A talented Dame for sure.

Susan Holthaus: my colleague and friend who has read and reread my drafts and then patiently made suggestions. Once an English teacher, always an English teacher. A loyal and trusted Dame.

Carrie Andersson: my beautiful daughter whose support and love I treasure. A DIT (a Dame in training—she's still young).

Pico, the Princess: my polka-dotted rescue mutt and inspiration for Miss Dot, Susan's companion. A Dame in need of a depilatory.

Arline Chase: my editor and publisher who graciously decided to take a chance on an "old" English teacher and the *Toby Martin* series. Now she has come out of "retirement" to take a chance on the Dames. A brave Dame indeed.

Lee Johnson: my cheerleader, sometimes research assistant, reviewer, dear friend, and main squeeze. You are officially admitted into the Dames Club.

About Barbara Grengs

Barbara Grengs is a retired English teacher who reads, writes, gardens, and knits. She currently resides in Roseville, Minnesota with her two dogs.